D1201127

THE MAGIC GARDEN

THE
MAGIC
GARDEN

Gene Stratton-Porter

The American Reprint Company

MATTITUCK

Republished by Special Arrangement
with Doubleday and Company, Inc.

Library of Congress Cataloging in Publication Data

Porter, Gene Stratton, 1863-1924.
  The magic garden.

  Reprint of the 1st ed. published by Doubleday, Page,
Garden City, N. Y.
  SUMMARY: A wealthy young girl spends her youth
preparing for the return of a young man she has loved
since childhood.
  I. Title.
PZ7.P8318Mag15   [Fic]   76-41378
ISBN 0-89190-942-7

AMERICAN REPRINT, a division of
The American Reprint Company/Rivercity Press
Box 1200
Mattituck, New York 11952

Manufactured in the United States of America

Contents

THE MAGIC GARDEN

PART ONE

Little Hungry Heart

Little Hungry Heart

"AMARYLLIS," said Nurse Benson, "without exception, you are the naughtiest child that God ever made."

Amaryllis sneaked a cake of floating soap from the bathtub, set it on the marble floor under cover of her nightie, pressed a very plump pink foot firmly on it, then skated across the room, coming up with sudden impact against the wash bowl opposite. If Benson wanted to use the soap again, naturally, she must recover it.

Amaryllis turned and made up what was intended to be an ugly face. A side glance in a mirror showed her that it was not nearly so repulsive as she wanted it to be, so by pulling down the corners of her eyes and pulling up the corners of her mouth with her fingers and sticking her tongue slightly farther out, she highly improved the effect she desired to attain.

Then she straightened her face back to its usually lovely lines, looked up at her nurse, and calmly explained, "That wasn't for *you*. I made that one up for God."

Nurse Benson was very properly shocked—but not beyond words.

"If you are as naughty as that," she said firmly, "God will let a policeman get you."

To which Amaryllis answered promptly, "I'd lots rather have a policeman get me than God."

Nurse Benson retrieved the soap and cleansed it.

"Don't you love God?" she inquired reprovingly.

Then Amaryllis, without the help of lifted mouth corners and down-drawn eyes, achieved facial expression so full of rebellion that Nurse Benson was very properly shocked again. Amaryllis fixed covetous eyes on the soap. She loved skating across the floor on wet soap. It was a worthy achievement to make the soap slip on the floor and to keep herself from slipping from the soap.

"No, I just *hate* God," she said deliberately.

"I am going to tell your father," said Nurse Benson emphatically. "The very first time he comes, I'm going to tell him."

"I wish you would," said Amaryllis. "I just wish you would! I'm going to tell him myself the first time I see him, and I'm going to tell him I *hate* him worser than I hate God!"

"I am just *amazed* at you!" said the nurse. "A

beautiful little girl like you, in a lovely home like this, with everything that your heart could wish!"

Amaryllis clenched a pair of small hands tight and elevated a small chin, and out of the depths of her heart, tried to the utmost limits of exasperation, she screamed at the top of her voice, and screamed, and screamed, and kept on screaming until she was exhausted.

Then she backed against the edge of the bathtub and, with distorted face and small hands beating, with small lips quivering, and heart thumpings showing through her nightrobe, she shouted, "God is for little girls whose fathers stay at home, and whose mothers love them, and whose big brothers aren't taken away from them! God only loves little girls when their *mothers* love them!"

Nurse Benson shut her mouth tight and walked across the room. Finally she turned and said patiently, "Please, Amaryllis, won't you let me bathe you now?"

Instantly Amaryllis marched up to her, dropped relaxed hands, lifted her quivering chin, and said very politely, "Yes, ma'am."

So there was no more trouble that morning. But there had been trouble previous mornings, and there would be trouble mornings to come, and what the end of it was going to be Nurse Benson could not foresee.

A year ago, when she had come to take charge of a

very beautiful little girl who had big, wide-open, sky-blue eyes and hair like sunburned gold all tumbling in soft wavy curls over her head, a red mouth, and a pink rose-leaf skin, she had thought it very likely that she had fallen into a pleasant job. Then, almost before a cat could wink its eye, Nurse Benson had discovered that she had been very carefully selected and very carefully trained concerning her job for the sole purpose of having the child placed, so far as its physical welfare was concerned, in her hands alone. For the child's mental welfare there was a governess who was supposed to teach her English, and another governess who came two hours a day and was certainly supposed to teach her French. There was a housekeeper to see that the big house was forever immaculate and shining, and down in the kitchen there was a cook to prepare delicious food. In the front hall there was a man who was a footman when he opened the door and who turned into a butler when he served the food. The double office damaged his feelings considerably but, since there was only one small girl in the family he served, he had to summon all his courage and carry off the damage with as high a head as he could negotiate. The sop to his pride lay in the fact that he was paid more for the double office than he would have been had he occupied either position alone. And there was more sop in the fact that he was not the only man on the premises who lived in a glass house. There

was another man who suffered wounded feelings because he had to feed a couple of dogs and curry a
pony in addition to performing the duties of a chauffeur. Naturally, it was beneath the dignity of a chauffeur who drove a Rolls-Royce with a monogram on
the door to curry a pony and feed dogs, but there
were times when Amaryllis came out on the lawn
and played with the dogs, since she had nothing else
in the world that was alive to play with except the
dogs. Sometimes she rode the pony. And because
added to the customary wages of a chauffeur, there
was a bonus for currying and feeding and various
other attentions, discreet and silent truce was main-
tained between the man in the front hall and the
man in the garage. They were so scrupulously polite
to each other that, if she had listened to them,
Amaryllis would not have needed another particle of
training on the subject of politeness, for they used
wonderfully correct speech.

The arrangement all began, so far as the workers
about the house knew, right out of a clear sky. They
had thought that Paul Minton was staying at his club
and in town a very great deal because he had an unusual rush of business. They had thought that Mrs.
Minton was spending most of her time with her
dressmakers and shopping in preparation for the
months she spent every year somewhere across the
ocean. And then, just like that—they had been informed that Paul Minton was remaining at his club,

while Mrs. Minton's trunks were packed and, with a hasty kiss for each of her children, she had started for her boat.

So far as the servants could see, and so far as Amaryllis and her little big brother Peter could see, the family was split quite as evenly as if it had been done with a very large, very sharp knife. Peter and everything pertaining to him was packed up and carried twenty miles away and set down in a house fully as big and even more prosperous and having larger numbers of useless people standing round than were in the home that was left for Amaryllis.

Peter was informed that he was the property of his father and that hereafter whatever he wanted he must ask his father about, while all the money that had been left him by his grandfather would be kept for him until he was thirty years of age. In the meantime, he must study hard with his tutors; and when he was old enough, he might go abroad; and when the time came he could have polo ponies, and yachts and everything that money can buy. Amaryllis was five and Peter was ten. Since they never had been trained to take the slightest interest in each other, it did not make so very much difference to either of them when the day came for their separation.

Peter's house was finer and larger, and he had more people to take care of him than Amaryllis had. Personally, Amaryllis liked her house better than she liked Peter's. From the time she could remember, Peter had been on her landscape, largely to her discomfort. He was rough and stronger than his little sister. He pushed her; he snatched things from her hands if he happened to want anything she was playing with. He liked to frighten the pony she was riding until it reared and threw her. He used to whistle sharply for the dog she was playing with, and he laughed unrestrainedly when she got a hard fall. Because he never had been thrown from a horse or the back of a big dog and cracked against the stones and walks himself, he had no idea how it hurt. He was the elder, and no one ever had done those things to him.

Peter was not any worse than any other boy who had lived for ten years in a house with a father and mother and a big flock of helpers, and had never had any of the right kind of attention from any of them. Whatever the women who bathed and dressed Peter could succeed in teaching him—if any of them happened to be the kind of a woman who would teach a little boy what his mother should teach him—whatever the men who were supposed to teach him, whether of sports or of books, could induce him to learn, Peter knew. But he had never been taught anything by his father, he had not gotten the right kind of exercise, nor had the right kind of food; and he had not grown into a big, fine boy with the pink cheeks and bright eyes that his father's son should have had. Peter was a little fellow with a very round head and a prim mouth and chin—not so very much chin—and cheek bones a trifle high. He had learned to speak correct English, but he spoke it slowly. His temper was not bad. The greatest defect there was about Peter was that he had lived for ten years without love. That was what was the matter with Amaryllis. But she had lived for only five years without love.

So when the big knife, wielded by the judge of the divorce court, came cutting its way through the Minton family, there were four people left to face life under different conditions.

Mr. Minton faced it from a club and from an apartment in the big city near by to which he sent his personal belongings. He swore by everything holy that never again in all this world could anyone induce him to marry, not even an angel straight out of heaven, still clad in white and having feathery wings and a big harp. He said all the angels he had ever seen pictured were women, and none of the women he knew were angels, and if heaven were full of angels, how did they get there? And he was tired of paying for feathers, and as for harping, he'd had enough to last him if he lived as long as Methuselah.

Mrs. Minton headed for the dock and straight across the sea because there were lords that she loved to play with in England, and there were counts in France, and dukes in Italy, and Spain was full of romance, and there were sheiks across the Mediterranean that really were good sport; and since she had more money than she could spend, and since she was still young, and since she was undeniably beautiful, why in all this world should she not develop her individuality and amuse herself according to her tastes and the desires of her heart? She asked all her friends "Why not?" and as most of them had done just what she was proposing to do, all of them said, "Why not, indeed?" When her boat left its moorings, she felt that she had done her whole duty. She had tried very particularly to install a capable woman as housekeeper for Amaryllis. She had had a doctor carefully examine the nurse in whose charge she left the child. She had tried the brand of French of the French governess and found it quite as good as her own. She had read a tiresome number of credentials concerning this governess. She knew the house was warm and contained every known luxury. She had given birth to Amaryllis. She had found numbers of people anxious to take care of her. Why should she be tied further?

That disposed of two of the Minton family.

It left Number Three, which was Peter. He came next because he was a boy, the elder, and for these excellent reasons he had been bequeathed by his grandfather a million or two more than his little sister. The grandfather who had left him the money had wanted to make sure that Peter did not miss anything. He had been convinced all his days that he had missed something. He was not sure what, but whatever it was, he was stubbornly set on having little Peter make up in his life what his defrauded grandfather had missed while he earned the millions that constituted the deepest misery of these two help-less children. Grandfather was sure that men needed more money than women, so Amaryllis had heard it said that Peter had more money than she. Peter, a solemn little figure with a grave face, the limit in clothing, and only Heaven knew what in his heart, ate when it was mealtime, slept when it was bedtime, had his lessons on the schedule laid down by the tutor, and for the remainder of the day devoutly wished that he were dead. Because Peter was quite the lonesomest boy that the big island on which he lived ever contained. He was the rich man's son. There were millions in the bank that were his. He had an allowance that he could not spend to save his little soul, because everything he really needed that could be bought in stores and markets was provided for him. Peter did not know what in the world to do with the money that he was expected to spend. He carried it until his pockets got full, and some of it he gave to anybody who happened to come his way looking as if they wanted money. Sometimes he rode his horse, or drove in his car to the home of the one other boy not so far from where he lived, who pitied his loneliness and sometimes asked him to come to his house. At that home Peter really had a good time.

That fortunate boy lived in a house where the father and mother were polite to each other. They had a way of coming down the stairs with their arms around each other. They were very tall and very handsome, and their son was tall and handsome, too. He was a generous boy with a kind heart, and he knew all about how lonely little Peter was, and he very obligingly showed him how to spend considerable of his money. Peter was tickled nearly to death to spend the money, because in return for it he got at that house what he had no place else on earth—a peep into a real home, a vision of real love. He met a man who asked him about his dogs and horses and his cars, and treated him as if some day he were going to be a man worth while. He met a woman who asked him about his lessons and what he had to eat and what he had to play with, and who made him presents of wonderful games and gave him books, perfectly wonderful books, full of stories of knights and warriors and great achievements, stories about sailors and soldiers and a big world that Peter thought he really would go out and see when he grew older, if he were not too badly bored to make a start.

But Amaryllis was not so fortunate. She was not big enough to go to visit any of the neighbors alone, and there did not happen to be any neighbors very near who had liked the kind of a woman that Amaryllis' mother had been. They were not her friends. So when she was gone, they were not friendly to the little girl left in the big house. Five years is not very old, and yet there are many things that five years of wide eyes and alert ears can learn. The most that Amaryllis knew she had gathered from nurses, governesses, chauffeurs, butlers, and cooks, and a very large per cent of it she had learned by listening —just walking up softly and keeping quiet when people did not know she was around. So Amaryllis knew the very dreadful things that could be said about a mother who would not stay married to a very fine man who did not do a thing worse than any man of his age and position and wealth was doing, a man who would come home and who would take care of his family and who would behave himself if he got any encouragement. Amaryllis knew, because of what she had heard the helpers say, that her father had never had any encouragement to do anything except keep away from home. No one in the whole house liked her mother, and everyone did like her father. At least, they were afraid of him, they obeyed him, and they did not deride him when his back was turned.

Amaryllis' case happened to be particularly bad because the big knife that cut through her family put her father and brother on one side of the family and left her brother in her father's care, and after a manner, her father did take care of her brother. At least, he was only forty miles away and could come in an hour if he were really needed. That he was really needed every day, he refused to concede. About one day a month was his limit.

On the other side, this big knife had put Amaryllis in her mother's care. And the one thing Amaryllis knew above every other thing was that her mother refused to care. Every day of her life the lonely little girl went down to the big bronze gates and, sometimes with a dog beside her, stood and looked through the panels locked above her head that shut her in from the world outside. She watched for cars rolling by with little girls in them, and she could see by looking in her mirror that they did not have half such tumbly, silky, yellow curls, that their eyes were not so big and wide open, that their cheeks were not so pretty, and that their dresses were not half so fine as hers. But through the bars of that gate, she had seen wonderful things happening to other fortunate little girls. Sometimes a little girl rode by standing on her knees with her arms around the neck of a beautiful woman and her face laid against her cheek. The woman's arms would be around the little girl, and they would be smiling. Sometimes they would be romping in the car as if it didn't make a particle of difference if hats were crooked and hair ruffled and cheeks and lips sticky with kisses. Sometimes the little people would be asleep and their heads would be laid over against their mother's shoulder, and there would be robes tucked around them and arms to support them and faces to look down at them—faces all aglow and alight with the kind of smiles on which little children grow and flourish.

When Amaryllis could not stand the things she saw through the gate any longer she would go slowly up the wide walk and around the house and back to the garage. Sometimes she would play with the dogs awhile, sometimes she would ride the pony up and down the drive awhile, and at times the chauffeur would tell her a story about when he was a little boy. A few times he had played marbles with her. Sometimes she would coax the gardener to tell her stories about when he lived across the sea in a cold land where they had to work very hard to have even a few flowers and a little fruit in summer. But he would not bring his children to play in the garden while he worked. She had begged him and begged him; she had even ordered him to bring them; but before her orders stood very strict orders from her mother. He was not to carry in mumps and measles and whooping cough and things that Amaryllis thought it would be lovely to have if she could be all tucked up in bed and have a mother to hold her and put a sympathetic face against her cheek and say little murmury things to her. She would not have minded having almost anything you could mention if it could have been mitigated only a little bit with love and individual care.

So it is very easy to understand—what with the

things that Amaryllis saw through the gates and learned at the stables and heard about the house, and taking into account the things that she was *not* taught, and taking into account the impersonal manner in which were imparted to her the things she *was* taught—it is very easy to realize that there came times when Amaryllis clenched her fists and stuck her chin in the air and screamed at the top of her voice. But the trouble was that, as the days went on, in the absence of anyone in fixed authority, all the helpers in the house began to think more and more about themselves and to pay less and less attention to the little girl. So months passed, with things going that way, which makes it very easy to see that the little heart in the body of Amaryllis and the small brain at the base of her skull were getting very badly warped. Almost anything you could mention connected with home life was going just exactly the way that it should not go if a fine specimen of feminine childhood is to evolve into a woman who is going to found a home and be able to do something for her family and her neighbors and her country, and maybe something that God up in heaven would be pleased about as well.

Everyone in the house knew that the times when Amaryllis screamed were becoming more and more frequent. Everyone in the house knew perfectly well that it was very bad indeed for Amaryllis when her little nerves grew all jangled and her heart rebelled and her brain got all mixed up, when she clenched her fists and screamed and screamed until she could not scream any longer.

The servants talked it over among themselves and said someone should write to her mother, and they said someone should tell her father. They all agreed that there should be someone in the house of the child's age for her to play with. But not one of them wrote the letter, or risked losing a place by telling, or found a child to come to play, because another child meant slightly more work for them, and the less work they had to do for Amaryllis and the more time they had to spend on their own concerns, the better they enjoyed themselves. And, after all, Amaryllis was not *their* child, and if her father would not come to see her more than once a month, and if her mother went away and left no plans about coming back, why should they shoulder more responsibility and work?

So it came to be the custom when Amaryllis screamed that everyone walked away and left her to scream, and it was not much fun screaming when there was no one to listen to her scream, and it did not do a particle of good. So gradually Amaryllis stopped screaming and started thinking. The thoughts that worked out of her brain were far too old and too deep and too intricate for five years of childhood. She soon found out that there was only one way for her to get through the gates. If she watched her chance and found a telephone when no one could hear her and called Peter and asked if she might come, and if Peter said that he was at home and that she might, then the big car would come to the door at her command, and Amaryllis, dressed in her loveliest clothes, would ride in state to visit Peter. Sometimes she had dinner with him and did not go home until it was dark. Sometimes he allowed her to play with the new games he had. Sometimes they talked over the manner in which they lived, and both of them knew that they were so lonesome and so hungry for love and for other children to play with, and for the things that all children really in their hearts want to do, that neither of them could find words to express exactly what they thought or what they truly felt.

Once Amaryllis said, "Peter, does Father ever take you to a circus or to a ball game?"

Peter shook his head, because he was a man of few words.

"Wouldn't you like just to sit in his car while he plays polo or golf?"

Peter nodded his head.

"Won't he *ever* take you?"

Peter shook his head.

"For goodness sakes!" cried Amaryllis. "Open your mouth, Peter! Open your mouth and say something, or I'll begin to scream!"

"Scream if you want to," said Peter. "I don't care!"

"For goodness sakes!" said Amaryllis again. "What do you want me to scream for? At my house when I scream everybody goes away and shuts the doors."

Peter thought that over a while and then he said very slowly, "When you scream, something inside of me screams with you, and afterward I don't feel quite so tight and hard."

For the third time Amaryllis said it in exasperation.

"For goodness sakes, Peter! Is there a place inside of you that's tight and hard *all* the time?"

Peter nodded his head slowly.

Amaryllis laid down the engine she was trying to make run and walked over to Peter. She laid her hands on his knees and looked up at him.

"Peter," she said, "we haven't got anything in the world but just each other, have we?"

Then Peter the silent opened his mouth and asked, "How have we got each other? *We haven't!* There's twenty miles between us, and the court says you've got to stay in your house, and I've got to stay in mine. We *haven't* got each other. We haven't got anything we *want,* and I don't know what you wish, but I wish that I was dead!"

Peter arose, pushed Amaryllis away, turned his back, and went and stood and looked out of a window for a very long time. Amaryllis sat on the floor and tried to make the engine run, but she did not know how to work it. Peter would not do anything

but stand like a post and glare from the window, so
Amaryllis went quietly from the room and the house
and climbed into her car. She told her chauffeur to
take her for a ride, because Peter was cross and he
would not play and she did not want to go home until just time for dinner. She spoke bravely, but two
big tears squeezed out and rolled down her pink
cheeks and stained the wide ribbons of her big floppy
lace hat. The chauffeur was young and he was
mighty sorry for the little girl he served. He thought
things over. The time was late June and the roads
were like barn floors. He knew the big island from
end to end. He could not see any reason why he
should not do as he was told. So, as he started the
car, he said to Amaryllis, "Where do you want to
go?"

Amaryllis thought that over.

Then she said, "I'd like to go where it is like a
picture that has water running in it and children
wading in the water and little woolly sheep on the
bank and cows eating daisies in a meadow. I would
like to go to a place like that kind of a picture."

Maybe you would not think there was a place like
that on the big island, but there were several, and
the chauffeur knew about them. So he stepped on
the gas and the big car sped away with a soft purring
and throbbing in the engine, and it was not so very
long before they crossed a bridge and Amaryllis cried
excitedly for him to stop. There really was a brook

coming through a meadow, a brook in a great hurry, for the water roared under the bridge. It really went away back into a place that looked like a beautiful picture. Not very deep water, but it was eager water, racing and splashing in its hurry. You could see stones through it and little pebbly places. The chauffeur turned around and let down the window so Amaryllis could stand up at the car door and listen to the water roar. By and by, she spied a big, clean, nice, inviting, very friendly looking stone beside the brook, and she told the chauffeur that in her purse there was five dollars that her father had given her to buy what she wanted with, and if he would lift her over the fence and set her on that stone and let her sit there for an hour, she would give him the five dollars. He could sit in the car and watch her and see that nothing happened to her.

The chauffeur had a heart, and he wanted the extra five dollars. He thought the proposition over a long time. He could not see a reason against it. So he opened the door and lifted Amaryllis across the fence and watched her go to the stone and seat herself very demurely and lean over to look down into the water. Then he parked the car as close to the fence as he could get it, and for ten or fifteen minutes watched Amaryllis. Certainly Amaryllis watched him. From under the brim of her big hat she watched him with the sharpest pair of eyes that ever had been trained on him. She sat just as still as still. She did not let

herself lean over to look in the water to watch the
tiny little fish enough to worry him for fear she
might fall. She just sat and watched the little bits of
things not much longer than her fingers with little
black specks on their noses and little touches of red
paint on their sides as they darted around in the
quiet places. Bugs with long bodies and wings she
could see through came past. She never dodged, even
when she was afraid, because she was keeping so still.
Sometimes she turned her head and looked back to
see what was behind her. There was nothing there
except some nice cows eating grass and some white
sheep. She could see a path along the bank of the
brook that maybe had been made by the feet of little
children. She studied it closely and, sure enough, just
like the print of her foot on a fat soft cake of soap,
there was a footprint on the path. How fine! To put
bare feet on soft, black, friendly earth. Then under
her hat brim she watched the driver and, by and by,
a slow smile crept over her face because she saw his
head fall forward and then jerk up straight again.
He looked quickly to see if she were there, and there
she sat with her hands folded looking sedately at the
water.

The sun was shining and the birds were singing,
and there were not very many people passing. The
day was warm and the chauffer had been up until
very late the night before, so his head went forward
several times more and finally it dropped back and

rested against the cushion, and his shoulders relaxed. His hands slid from the steering wheel. Very softly Amaryllis stood up on the rock and looked at him and saw that he was sound asleep. That was exactly what she had hoped would happen when she promised him her five dollars. That was why she sat quietly on the rock when she was wild to chase butterflies, and gather daisies and, oh! that running, noisy, teasing, coaxing water!

Amaryllis got up and stood on the rock and looked down the footpath. It was just as bare and smooth as a floor, except for the footprints; and there were flowers, little white daisy flowers that she knew from pictures, and lots of other flowers that she did not know, and many kinds of bright birds, and it smelled something wonderful. No one had mowed the grass. No one had trained the flowers until they looked like dead things. It was all mussy, and things grew where they pleased, and birds sang as they pleased and flew where they would. Sometimes they came down and splashed in the water, and when they did that Amaryllis decided that splashing in that water would beat any bathtub in all this world, and if flowers grew as they liked and birds and sheep and cows were free, why should a little girl be locked behind big lonely gates?

So Amaryllis stood up and she looked hard at the tumbling water of Roaring Brook. She looked at the path of alluring invitation, she looked at the sky so serene and smiling, then she listened to the birds, singing to split their throats. Then she looked at the driver and remembered the money she had promised him. A long time she had planned and waited for her hour of freedom. Now it had come. There was not a living soul to say, "Amaryllis, don't!" There were the flowers beckoning "Come," the birds crying "Come!" the little fish daring her—"Chase me!" A long, long time she had waited for such a chance. Today she had made her chance, so just as still as a faint breath of air, Amaryllis climbed the fence and slipped back to the car. Why she did this was because she was a dead game little sport. For weeks she had waited—this was her first opportunity—but she had made a promise. She was forced to go back to the car.

The bank was very steep and it was hard to reach the running board on that side, so softly on tiptoe, she slipped around to the other side and climbed up. She worked until she got the back door of the big car open and, stepping in, she reached into the driver's compartment and dropped the money she had promised him on the seat beside him. That was Amaryllis. If she told Benson she would hold still and be good while she was bathed, she did it. Whatever she said she would do, that thing she did.

Today she was going to put the first stain on her record. She was not going to keep her whole promise. She had told the driver that she would stay on the rock and she had not intended to do so when she told him, because that day the ache in her side was so very dreadful, and Peter had not been the slightest help. In fact, Peter had not done a thing but make it worse because, as far as Amaryllis could see, Peter was more helpless than she was. She knew that he was twice as old as she was. She had heard it often enough. But Peter looked hungrier and lonelier than she did. There had been a nice engine. They could have had some fun with it if Peter had gotten down on the floor and played; but Peter only stood at the window and looked across the big island to the one spot where he ever had a good time, and remained grumpy.

So Amaryllis had at last a chance to work out a thought that for a long, long time had been hidden in her heart. She felt slightly sorry for the chauffeur as she laid the money beside him and closed her purse with her hanky and her small change in it. She thought very likely they might scold him when he went back home without her, but that could not be helped, because home (when there was nobody in it but one little girl and a number of big people who were so selfish that they did not care what became of that little girl so long as she was alive) was not a place that did anything but make a big, hard spot in your left side and a big, hard place you could not swallow down in your neck.

Just as still as thistle seed on the wind, Amaryllis

turned, ever so tiptoe softly, to step from the running board to the road, and as she lowered herself,
one of the big blue loops of ribbon on her floppy hat
caught over the latch and tore the tie loose at one
side. In an effort to save the hat, Amaryllis dropped
her purse. She had some little difficulty disentan-
gling the ribbon. When she finally got it loose, she
was so frightened for fear a car would come whizzing
down the road or the driver would wake up and her
beautiful scheme would be spoiled that her little
hands trembled. With the ribbon loose at one end,
she could not tie the hat on her head. Neither could
she hold it while she climbed the fence. What difference did it make whether she wore a hat or not?
There were boxes of them in all colors at home. In
desperation she threw it as far into the middle of the
road as she could, while she never thought of the
purse.

But with this picture clear in your mind, it is easy
to see what the chauffeur thought when he awakened
and Amaryllis was not on the rock, while the back
car door on the street side was open, and before it
lay a little purse, and in the street lay a torn, floppy
little hat.

Amaryllis slid down the embankment, and oh,
so softly and easily she took her ruffled dress over the
fence, and on tiptoe and looking back until she was
very sure that she was not going to be seen, she
reached the little path, the nice, black path that had

the imprints of children's bare feet on it, the path that seemed to lead back into a land the like of which Amaryllis never had seen.

Once she was past the stone, she clutched her skirts on both sides and lifted them high, and down that path she went as fast as her legs could carry her. They were rather sturdy legs, and they could carry her quite a distance. Down that path she went as fast as she could race, and when she grew tired at last and her breath began to come in short gasps, she sat down and rested a while. The farther she went, the thicker the bushes became, while the little path was not so well traveled as it had been. But it was still a path. She could make her way. The sun kept on shining, the birds cried "Come on! Come play with us!" There was not a soul anywhere to say, "Amaryllis, *don't!*"

It would not have made any difference if there had been, because this was the thing that Amaryllis had been planning for a long, long time. She intended to run away from everyone. She had planned for months to beat those barred gates. She was going to go on and on, until she found some house that looked friendly, that had a mother in it. She was going to go into it and knock on the door and, in her very prettiest party way, she was going to ask the people if, please, they didn't want a very good little girl at their house?

The one thing that bothered Amaryllis was where

the house was going to be. As far as she could see, there was not any house, and a marshy place was coming into the stream. It was a land of wonder in the marshy place. There were yellow flowers and there were red flowers and blue flowers. There were more birds and there were great velvet butterflies. Oh, it was a wonderful place! Amaryllis went on more slowly, and the nice path led around the edge of the marshy place and went right back on the bank of the singing brook again. Here the brook was prettier than it had been below the marsh. The water was clearer and the bed was rougher, so the water roared louder and laughed and chuckled.

Amaryllis sat down and pulled off her shoes. She did not pay much attention to where she threw them or to where she threw her socks. Then she slipped down the bank and set her little feet, velvet soft and tender—the little feet that never had touched the earth before in all her life—she set them bare right down on the creek bank. The feel of it was the most delightful thing, so soft and cool. The narrow green blades of grass dropped over and tickled them. Two or three steps, and she kicked her toes in the water. It was the greatest fun! Then she stepped in on a pebbly place and let the water run over her toes. That made her dance and squeal for joy. She had to be careful not to fall. So she held her skirts on each side and followed out the little pebbly shoal and stood still. The sun smiled down on her and the birds sang for her, and, oh! how that water did sing! Back up a way it came roaring over a fall, and it laughed and chuckled about it, and then it swirled out into a deep pool where more of the tiny fishes were. Then it straightened up and came right down toward her and went between two big stones and said, "Glug! Glug! Glug!" Amaryllis stuck the tip of her little pink tongue out then and said, "Glug! Glug! Glug!" after it. That was fun! Water beat Peter all hollow. Water would talk to her! So she stood there kicking her toes in the water to make it splash and mocking what it said and laughing for pure joy.

Then she heard something. Something coming. It seemed as if it were coming down the brook, and yet it could not be coming down the brook, because what she heard was music. Amaryllis knew about music. She had seen people play pianos and harps and violins. She had heard bands and orchestras. She knew about the instruments that you blew in one end and wonderful tones came out of the other. Her governess played tunes on the piano for her to dance to. She knew what this music coming toward her was. Times when her mother had been having a party, men, or sometimes women, standing beside the grand piano in the music room, had played on violins. She knew a violin, but she had never heard a violin played the way this one was being played. This violin played like sunshine and flowers in bloom. Sometimes it stayed in the same place quite a while. When a bird up on a branch very carefully said "Pee-a-wee! Pee-a-wee!" right after it the violin said the same thing. When a lamb across the meadow said "Baa-a-a-ah!" the violin said "Baa-a-a-ah!" too. That was a joke—making a violin talk like a bird and baa like a sheep.

Amaryllis stepped from the shoal and started up the stream to find the violin that sounded like magic. It was rather rough going. Some of the stones that looked so perfectly nice to step on were not nice at all. Something slippery was on the tops of them that tried to throw her down, but walking on soap at home had been good practice. She never fell once. The pebbly places were the safest, but there were not always pebbly places to step on, and sometimes she just had to step on the slippery rocks to get ahead. The bushes and shrubs were coming more thickly—willows and elders and button bushes and all sorts of things that Amaryllis never had seen before, at least not to be right next to them and to touch them with her fingers. But because she was going upstream and the violin was coming downstream, it was not so very long before she found it.

Amaryllis' mouth fell open and her eyes grew very wide because, when she found the violin, she found something else she had not reckoned on. She had thought maybe it was a magic violin that was floating through the air and playing tunes all by itself the way the water sang gay tunes, and the birds sang glad notes, and the flowers made little waves of color music. So when Amaryllis got her first sight of the violin, her mouth fell open the widest it ever had, and her eyes grew the biggest and roundest they had ever been, because that violin was right out in the middle of the brook, and that violin was in the hands of a boy, and the boy had a head as black as the blackest wing on the blackest blackbird that came down to the brook to bathe and drink. He had eyes big and round and wide open and almost as black as his hair, while his cheeks were a soft, creamy color, and there were splashes of red in them. His mouth was wide and friendly, and his teeth were even and white. He was tall and slender. He must have been three or four years older than Peter. He wore a gray shirt and gray linen trousers rolled up above his knees and held up with a belt at his waist. His feet were bare and he was standing in the water.

He was looking up at the sky and all around him, and every note that a bird sang, and every "Moo-o" that a cow called, and every "Baa-a" that a sheep made, he repeated on the violin. Sometimes he would look down at the brook and make the violin laugh and chuckle and leap down a steep place and whirl out into a shallow pool and chuckle between stones and warble over pebbles. It was the funniest thing. Nothing like it ever had been done before in all the world—not in any pictures in all the stacks of picture books of which Amaryllis was dead tired.

Then, standing there in a pause, when the birds had forgotten and the sheep were quiet, the boy began to play his own music. But Amaryllis did not like what he played then, because the notes he made were the thoughts that were in her brain spoken on a violin, when worst of all she wanted to sit on somebody's lap and lean her head on somebody's breast. Amaryllis had gotten to the place where she did not care the least little bit whose lap she sat on, or whose breast pillowed her, just so it was someone that *wanted* a little girl, someone who loved all little children. So when the notes grew so lonesome and so hungry that they told Amaryllis that this boy wanted to sit on someone's lap and put his arms around someone's neck and kiss someone, Amaryllis started bravely through a rather deep place right up Roaring Brook toward the boy.

When he heard her and looked down at her and took the violin from beneath his chin and smiled at her, Amaryllis walked up to him and held out her hand. In a rough little voice, because of the hard spot in her throat, she said to the boy, "Haven't you got anyone to love you, either?"

The boy looked down at her and said, "Not today."

Amaryllis looked up at him and said, "Then I'm worse off than you, because I haven't anyone any day."

Amaryllis was very wild-rose pink and sky blue and sun gold, and she'd had splendid luck about not falling into the water on account of experience with soap in the bathtub. Her petticoat and her ruffly dress billowed out around her. There was not a head of goldenrod in the swamp, nor any gold flower any-where, that was one half so lovely as her head. The boy shifted the violin and the bow to one hand, and took Amaryllis's offered hand and, holding it very carefully, led her over to the bank. He looked at her from her dimpled pink feet to her dainty little hands and delicate face. He looked at the fineness of her exquisite clothes and he asked, "What's your name?"

Amaryllis looked at him and remembered a fairy story she had heard one time. She remembered some-thing else. She remembered that if she said, "My name is Amaryllis Minton," when the chauffeur woke up and found out that she had run away, some-one might put it in the papers the way the butler had said it was in the papers about her father and mother when the judge with the big knife divided up her family. So Amaryllis took refuge in the fairy story. She realized that she was being very bad. She had not kept her word about staying on the rock. That was hardly fair to the chauffeur. And now this nice boy, the very beautifullest boy she ever had seen in all her life, was asking her a question and she was not going to answer it true, because there was the fairy tale, and the fairy tale was the thing that was true. So when the boy asked, "What's your name?" Amaryllis answered what the boy might have thought was promptly, because Amaryllis had practiced thinking so much she could think very quickly indeed for five years old. What she answered was: "Little Hungry Heart."

The boy with the soft black eyes and the silky black hair many, many times curlier than Peter's hair, opened his mouth and his eyes wider still and stared at her, and as if he could not at all believe what he had heard, he repeated: "Little Hungry Heart?"

Then softly and gently he ran a hand down her chubby little legs and took the sole of her dimpled foot in one of his hands, and dazedly and tenderly he studied her.

"Little Hungry Heart?" he repeated, as if he could not at all believe what he had heard.

So Amaryllis resolved that she would make a clean breast of it, even if she did not know exactly what a clean breast was. She decided to tell the truth. So she said, "The big judge took a big knife and cut our family right spang in two. Peter belongs to Father and Father lives at the club, so Peter's standing at the window so lonesome he doesn't care if he dies. And I'm right here and Mother's away off across the ocean, and she doesn't like me at all. I daren't sit on her lap or put my arms around her neck or lay my head on her breast, and an old paid nurse takes care of me when I'm sick, and a nurse bathes me in the evening, and a governess teaches me, and there is no one to play with me and no place to go, and a house so big I'm afraid of it, and, oh, boy, what's *your* name? And if there isn't anyone to love you today, will there be someone to love you *tomorrow?*"

The boy laid down the violin and sat down on the embankment very deliberately. He gathered Amaryllis up and set her on his lap. He put one arm around her, and he leaned her head up against his breast, and the long, slender fingers of his other hand combed down through her shining hair again and again. His lips came down on the top of her head and he kissed her curls and kissed them. Then his loose hand slid down her arm and took one of her little hands and held it close.

He said, "My name is John Guido Forrester, and the reason I haven't anyone to love me today is because my father has gone away on a journey. He paints the most beautiful pictures in all the world. No one else can make the trees and the water and the clouds and the sky come true on canvas as he can. But sometimes people want him to come and live with them for a while and paint things that they own in their forests or in their meadows or their mountains, and they don't want a boy around, so I have to stay at home and keep house and wait until Father comes back. It is awfully lonely when I have to stay alone, because when Father is here we walk together

and we fish together and we hunt together, and he
tells wonderful stories and we read great books. We
have a grand time when Father's here. But he has
been gone so long, and I don't know when he is coming back."

Then Amaryllis looked up at John Guido and
asked, "Did the big judge——?"

John Guido shook his head quickly.

Very softly he said, "No! God. A long time ago
when I was only a little fellow. I can remember a
few times, in a soft dress like this of yours, with, oh,
such big eyes and such wavy black hair, high up on
a big stage so she looked a little bit of a person, my
mother sang songs to a world of people, and Father
sat in a box and held me tight and we cried because
it was so beautiful, and all the other people cried
with us. And sometimes they stood up and waved
their handkerchiefs and it was wonderful! Then,
when her songs were sung, we could slip through a
door and go back to her dressing room, and she
would hold us in her arms and kiss us nearly to
death. I can feel her kisses now. Then, all on a sudden, God needed her up in heaven to show the angels how to sing, and Father and I had to give her
up for a little while, but we have her picture, and
some of the notes she made in her songs I can do on
the violin because I can remember them. When I
grow bigger Father is going to take me back to her
country, and I am going to learn to play so I can

stand on a big stage and make the violin say the things she did, and I am going to make the people stand up and wave their handkerchiefs and have tears all running down their faces."

Amaryllis lifted her head and looked at the boy and asked, "Well, what do you want to make them cry for?"

The boy smiled at her and said, "I don't want to make them cry to hurt their feelings. It is good for people to cry because their hearts are full of happy tears. I only want to make them remember sunny days and laughter and love and Italy. What I want to do is to go back to Italy."

But Amaryllis was practical.

"What are you going to do right now until your father comes?" she asked.

"I am going home and get my supper," answered the boy. "Then I am going to practice my music lesson."

"All right," said Amaryllis. "I'll go with you."

John Guido looked at her with his big eyes and said, "Isn't your father going to come from the club, or isn't your mother going to come after you?"

Amaryllis shook her head.

"No," she said. "Father doesn't come from the club more than once a month, and Mother doesn't ever come at all any more. Neither of them cares where I am, so it will be all right for me to go with you."

But John Guido was older and he knew better than that. So he sat still and thought things over.

Then he said, "But there must be someone. There's got to be a nurse or a governess or someone."

Amaryllis answered with perfect logic. "I'm here, aren't I? I got away from them, didn't I? It doesn't make any difference to them where I am, or I couldn't be here, could I? I'm not *their* little girl. They don't want to hold me on their laps. They don't want to pat my hair. They don't want to bother with me. I'm *going* with you, John Guido. I want the kind of supper you eat, and I want to sit on your lap some more, and if I hadn't given away all the money I had, I'd give it all to you and the purse, too."

John Guido's arms tightened suddenly and right then and there kissed her hair again, and Amaryllis nestled up against his breast and turned up her little soft, sweet face and pulled down his head and offered him her baby lips instead. John Guido touched them lightly because he was afraid of anything so fine and so sweet, and in a voice that did not sound a bit like the voice he had been using he said, "You little darling! You little Hungry Heart darling! Where are your folks? Isn't there a grandmother, or an aunt, or a cousin, or someone?"

Amaryllis shook her head and said, "No. Not anyone at all. Not even Peter. I *went* to Peter first and he wouldn't play with me. He turned his back and stood in the window. That's honest and true. Peter's worse off than I am. He can't get along as well without being taken care of as I can."

Amaryllis stood up and reached her hand and said, "Come on, John Guido. Let's go to your house."

But because he was older John Guido stood still.

"I think," he said, "that we must go back down to the road and find your car."

Then Amaryllis lifted her chin and looked him in the eye and said, "John Guido, if you take me back down to the road and find my car and send me back to those nasty people that don't love me and don't belong to me, I'll get away again, and the next time I'll not give you a chance to take me back. I'll go where the water is deep, and I'll get right into it, and I'll stay there until the big fish eat me."

John Guido stood still and looked down at Amaryllis.

Then he said, "You really have a father?"

Amaryllis nodded her head.

"And he stays in the city and only comes once a month?"

Amaryllis looked him straight in the eye and said, "Sometimes he doesn't come for two or three months."

John Guido's eyes grew smaller and narrower. His face grew whiter and his lips tightened.

"And what about your brother who turns his back and won't play with you?"

Amaryllis still looked him straight in the eye and said, "That isn't Peter's fault. Peter isn't much older than I am. His heart is just as hungry as mine is, but he can't stand it quite as well as I can, because Peter hasn't got as much brains as I have, even if I am only five. I always could think of more things to do than Peter can. *Peter's no help.*"

Then said John Guido, "You've really got a mother off somewhere across the ocean who *could* come to you if she *wanted* to?"

Still looking deep in his eyes, Amaryllis said, "*Sure* she could come if she wanted to. She could come tomorrow, if she would. She doesn't want to be bothered. She wants beautiful dresses and beautiful times and big, fine men to take her places. I daren't touch her, not for anything. I might wrinkle her dress or muss her hair or make a mark on her face. Just one, on my nose, is all she kissed me when she went away forever, and all she said was: '*Be a good girl.*'"

Then Amaryllis stepped back and her little fists clenched tight and her chin lifted up. It was very quivery, and the little mouth was twisting and the big eyes were getting very hard and bright as she said, "John Guido, how's anybody going to 'be a good girl' with nobody in all this world to love them?"

And John Guido said, "God knows, Little Hungry Heart! I don't!"

Then Amaryllis made the most attractive suggestion.

She said, "Maybe if you would take me to your house and keep me two or three days until they all got good and scared, if anyone would be scared about me, maybe they would find out whether they love me or not, and if they did they would come and get me, and if they didn't, why, then, maybe, your nice father would love me, too, and let me go on the walks with you and catch the little fishes and play in the water."

Then Amaryllis smiled the most enchanting smile that ever she could conjure up when there were tears back in her eyes and a tremble on her lips. She smiled through the tears and looked hard at John Guido and waited.

The boy thought it over and said, "I think you are right. It would serve them just the way they deserve. If nobody's taking care of you enough to keep you from running away like this and coming past a swamp where you might have drowned yourself if you had gotten into the muck, if nobody cares enough about you to watch you any better than that, they ought to have a good scare. I think you are right about it. You come on with me. I can get you enough to eat to keep you alive, and I can take care of you all right, and we will let them get scared as long as there is any scare left in them, and maybe, after that, they will know better how to treat a little girl who needs her mother and her father and her brother."

John Guido reached down his hand, and Amaryllis laid hers in it and trotted along beside him, and so they went for a long, long distance.

PART TWO

The Magic Garden

The Magic Garden

THEY went so far that Amaryllis' feet became tender, because they had not ever touched bare paths before. By and by she shut her lips very tight, because she would not tell John Guido that her feet hurt. But she could not keep from limping, and finally he saw what the trouble was. So he knelt down and showed her how to climb on his back and put her arms around his neck and her feet against his sides. He took one of her feet in one of his hands and the violin and the bow in the other, and she was careful not to hug him so tight that she would choke him. She laid her soft warm face down beside his and rubbed her cheeks over his hair, and she smelled like flowers, and her laugh rippled like running water and oriole notes.

So going, John Guido came into a bit of meadow that belonged to his father, and then he left the water and followed a well-beaten path between trees of willow and bushes of elder and wild sweet briar, past tall red lilies. He went on and on and finally he came to a garden. It was the most wonderful garden in all the world because the flowers did exactly what they pleased. They seeded down and came up and seeded down again and ran into each other's arms and on past and scattered everywhere, and all the vines ran sprawling over the ground or climbed trees or ran on top of the fence; and all the bulbs spread and grew in clusters, and everything was wild and free. Instead of a big locked bronze gate, an old wooden one hung on one hinge, and it was just as wide open as it could get. Anyone could run through and reach the meadow. Then at the far end of the garden there was a house.

The minute Amaryllis saw it, she loved the house. It was not a big house at all. It was a low, flat house with a veranda running around it that needed loads of spindles in its railing. The steps needed straightening, and everything needed paint. The bushes were as wild as the garden, and the grass grew long and waved in the wind like hair. It was a quiet house, and a homelike house. You could see all of it without walking until you were tired.

Inside, it was a wonderful house. There was one big room that smelled of pipes and tobacco, and there was a wide fireplace with heaps of wood beside it, and there was a big piano. The boy laid the violin on top of that. There were easy chairs and shelves full of books all around the walls. On one side of this room there was a door leading to another room that was nearly all glass. In it there was a world of the most wonderful books, and pictures and more pictures. Some of them stood up on easels, and some of them hung on the walls, and many of them stood on the floor. Lots of them that stood on the floor turned their faces to the walls. It was a wonderful room one could never become tired of. There were doors that opened out of it into the garden and onto the back porch; and if you went along the back porch far enough, you came to the dining room, and next came the kitchen.

In the kitchen John Guido looked up at the clock and said, "When it is five, Marie will come to cook my supper, and I will tell her that I am awfully hungry and I want lots of supper. Then I will have enough for you, too."

Then John Guido stood still and thought things over.

He said, "But I will have to tell Marie to come and stay all night and sleep on the couch beside your bed, because a little girl has to have a governess or a nurse or somebody to undress her. You can have Father's bed and sleep in his room, and I will have my bed and sleep in my room."

Amaryllis said that was all right. *Now* what should they do? And how long would it be until five o'clock?

—because she was awful hungry right that minute. John Guido said there were two hours yet until five, and so he went to the cupboard and cut a slice of bread and put butter on it and honey from a honey-comb, and gave it to Amaryllis. Amaryllis sat upon the table with her little soiled feet hanging down and ate the bread and butter and drank a glass of milk and thought that it was a feast. The boy brought a basin and put her feet in it, and washed the stains from them, and the bruises. Then, with a soft towel, he wiped them dry and held them against his cheeks and kissed the rosy abused soles and said, "I'm so sorry, oh, I'm so sorry that you lost your shoes."

Amaryllis said she was not sorry that she had lost her shoes at all. She did not like to wear shoes. She wanted her feet on the ground like little children in pictures, and pretty soon her feet would get used to the ground, and then they would be tough like the boy's feet and they would not hurt any more. The boy went into his room and closed the door and left Amaryllis to eat her bread and honey.

By and by, when he came out, he was the most beautiful boy that Amaryllis had ever dreamed about. He wore dark blue velvet breeches, long ones, clear down to the floor, and a dark blue coat and a little blouse of gold silk with a collar that came out over the coat collar, and cuffs that turned up over the coat sleeves. There were shiny shoes of patent leather and gold stockings on his feet.

He washed all the honey and bread crumbs from Amaryllis's face and he said, "Now we must find a place to hide you if the searchers come to find you, because at your house they *need* to do without you for several days and then, after *that,* maybe they will be more careful of you."

So they looked all around to find a place to hide Amaryllis if a policeman came. It was the boy who found a grand place under the chair in the glass room where models sat when John Forrester wanted to paint a picture of a person. It was a big chair with a curtain draped over it, and behind it there were worlds of room for Amaryllis to slip in and sit down and keep so quiet that no policeman would ever think of looking for her there. Then John Guido closed the front gate and locked the front door. He told Amaryllis that he did not think there was much danger of policemen coming there to look for her, because they lived so far from the road, and other people owned the land between them and where men would be searching. He thought it would be perfectly safe for them to go to the garden to play.

So John Guido took Amaryllis by the hand and led her into the Magic Garden. They sat down in the striped grass, all white and yellow and green and lavender striped grass, grass such as Amaryllis never had seen anywhere before. They sat down under the syringa bush which arose above them, all so sweet and smelly, with wonderful white flowers that show-

ered petals down like snowfalls if they pushed against
it ever so lightly. John Guido took the grass blades
and he broke them off into different lengths and laid
them between his thumbs and stretched them tight.
Then he lifted his thumbs to his mouth and played
the queerest tunes on the grass blades. Amaryllis
laughed until the tears ran down her cheeks. She
held out her hands and the boy put little blades between her thumbs and pulled them up tight and
held them and showed Amaryllis how to set her red
lips and blow. When she made a little squeak she
thought it was as fine as the music that the boy had
made. So she kept hunting for other blades and making squeaky sounds on them between her thumbs
and laughing, while every few minutes she came
back to the boy and held up her little red rosebud
of a mouth and said very plaintively, "Please, Boy,
I'm hungry *again*."

John Guido took her in his arms and gave her the
very sweetest kiss that he could think up, exactly the
way he thought the nicest mother in all the world
would put a kiss on the lips of a little baby thing that
was all yellow curls and hungry eyes and deep
dimples and lacy ruffles. That tells you all you need
to know about the kind of a boy John Guido Forrester had been born to be and had been trained
into.

When the striped grass whistles lost their novelty,
John Guido took a knife from his pocket, opened the

big blade, and taught Amaryllis a wonderful game. So expertly he flipped the knife from each finger, and then from his knees, and from the back of his hand, and from his closed fist with the thumb extended, and off his elbow and over his shoulder and from the top of his head—so expertly he flipped it that he never cut himself or missed one throw. He taught her the exciting game with a knife, called "Mumble-ty-peg." Amaryllis was not a bit afraid of the blade; like the sporting little girl she was, she went at it and she tried so very hard that she did better than any little girl five years old would have done unless she did try very hard indeed. And when she lost the game she had to pull a little wooden peg from the ground with her teeth to punish her for making mis-takes.

Always, as they played, the boy with the big black eyes kept watch toward the front part of the house; he kept watch down the walk that they had come; he kept watch over toward the kitchen side of the house, because he said Marie lived over there and she might come any minute to cook their supper. Then he decided that, since he would need Marie to undress Little Hungry Heart, and to bathe her and sleep be-side her, he would have to tell her anyway. So he be-gan to try to think what he could tell her that would not make her tell the policemen, if they came hunt-ing a little lost girl. At last he thought out what would be best to tell Marie, and he went over to tell

her right away so she would not come and be sur-
prised. Before he left Amaryllis he hid her behind a
big clump of peonies that had run wild for goodness
knows how long—long enough for them to become
almost bushes. They completely covered the half-
scared little girl with green leaves and blooms,
blooms as big as her head and sweet, so sweet she
kept plunging her face with its big eager eyes deep
into them, until her nose got enough pollen on it to
make it yellow as her hair.

When John Guido came back, he said everything
was all right. Marie was a good sort. She was mighty
glad that his little cousin had come out from the city
to visit him so that he would not be so lonely, and
she would be glad to stay all night and take care of
her, and if anyone came around that had no business
there, she would send them right away.

Then the black-eyed boy and the blue-eyed girl
laughed and laughed and laughed until their sides
ached. They leaned against each other and laughed
because they had such a very good joke on the people
who had not cared enough about a little girl to keep
her from having a heavy spot in her heart and a big
lump in her throat. The black-eyed boy said he
would teach them what happened when they had no
love to give to the sweetest little girl in all the world.

Then John Guido commenced doing things that
were real magic. Over by the garden fence where the
tall hollyhocks grew he went and cut them—great

single blossoms of pink or of white. He went up to the house and brought down two or three glasses of water and a handful of broom straws. Then he went over to the grape arbor and picked some green grapes as big as the end of his first finger. He went to the honeysuckle and gathered honeysuckle trumpets, and to the striped grass and came back with long banners of grass. He went down into the garden where the tomatoes and cabbages and vegetables grew, and from the bean row he selected some bean pods that had beans in them that were nearly big enough to begin to harden. Then, sitting in the striped grass under the snowing syringa bush, with the glasses of water arranged on the walk in front of them, on one of the long stiff broom straws he stuck a nice round grape for a head. Then he stuck the straw clear through another for a body. Then he put on another to make the body long enough to tie the belt around. Into this he stuck some shorter straws for legs and he put a bean on the end of each straw for a little foot. The feet looked like tiny Dutch wooden shoes. Then he took a hollyhock and with his knife carefully cut away the stamens and the pistil and trimmed off the calyx and then removed the grape head and the first section of the body and stuck the straw through the pink skirt he had made, a skirt that would barely let the little bean feet show beneath it. He fixed another hollyhock the same way and put back the body grape for a waist, and then he put on the head grape. Between the two body grapes he made a sash of striped grass. He made arms with little bits of broom straws stuck through honeysuckle trumpets so the little tubes made sleeves. He reached up to the syringa above him and got a blossom that was just opening. He cut the stem off, carefully cut the pistil out, and with a tiny little bit of straw he set it at a jaunty angle on the head of the little flower lady he was making. It made a lovely hat. Then he took his knife and made eyes and a nose and mouth. Such long, slender fingers the boy had, and he was so very skillful with them that soon the loveliest little lady you ever saw, all dressed up in pink and white, went into one of the glasses of water to keep her fresh.

Then Amaryllis went racing through the garden to gather every flower that she could find. Next the boy made an Italian lady with red and yellow hollyhocks, all gay and gorgeous. They cut away all the green from a long blade of grass to make her a sash of yellow. It was wonderful work, so dainty and so careful he had to be. When the little Italian lady was finished and put in her glass of water to live and the boy asked what kind of a lady she wanted next, Amaryllis thought a while, and then she made a suggestion.

"Make me," she said. "Make just me!"

The boy looked at her for a long time and then he said, "Little Hungry Heart, you are so sweet there isn't a flower in the garden sweet enough to make

you with, but if you are what you want, I will try.
But this time I must be very careful. I must do something different. You hunt through the striped grass
and see how near you can come to finding blades that
are all white, because they are the only things for
sashes and ribbons. Hunt away back in the shade
where it is damp and dark. The blades come whiter
because there isn't much light. Then search the
honeysuckles and see if you can find some, back in
the dark, that are whiter, too."

Then the boy went to one side of the garden, and
from tall stems he cut white lilies, Madonna lilies
that were like wax. He went to the rosebushes and
cut petals of silk. For Amaryllis he did not use a
green grape for a head. He tucked her behind the
syringa bush where she nestled down and solemnly
swore across her heart not to move for fear a policeman might see her, while he raced through the garden and down the path through the meadow and
came back with white balls from the button bushes
all golden with pollen over them. With his knife he
worked the pollen away from the space for a face.
He worked in a teeny bit of blue from the ragged
robins to make eyes, and he worked in a touch of
red from a salvia to make a mouth. The pollen he
left for hair. Then with the white lilies and the rose
petals and the button-bush head and the faded
honeysuckles for sleeves and the white-striped grass
for a sash, he made the handsomest little lady that

ever was made in all this world from broom straws and green-grape bodies and button heads from button bushes, and lilies. Amaryllis clapped her hands and patted him and kissed his cheeks and told him that she loved him better than all the world, she loved him better than anything up in the sky or down on the earth. Better than her hands, or her feet, or her eyes, she loved him.

The boy worked very soberly and constantly watched down the footpath into the meadow and across the garden to the corner of the house so he would not lose her. In the back of his head he determined that he would not go out on the road in three days and tell someone passing in a car that there was a little lost girl at his house, as he had thought at first he would do perhaps the next day. She might stay just as long as ever he could hide her, because never in his life had he done anything that he so loved to do as he loved taking care of Amaryllis. She *was* a little Hungry Heart. She had not told him stories about herself. Hunger was back deep in her eyes. Hunger was in her little hot, clutching hands. Hunger was on her thirsty lips. She *was* a little Hungry Heart, but it almost broke his tender boy heart to call her that.

So he said to her, "If I promise sure and certain to hide you as long as I can, to make them hunt and hunt until they get good and ready to love you hard, and to be tickled to pieces to see you come home

again, will you tell me what your really truly name
is?"

Little Hungry Heart thought that over only a
second. It was so reasonable. The boy was so convincing. She knew that he would do exactly what he
said he would. His lips were medicine on her little
bruised feet and her unloved hair and on her hands,
and when she made him kiss her, she adored his
light, gentle kisses. She would not have cared if he
had made them lots longer, and lots hotter, and
much harder. She had wanted to be loved so very
badly for such a long time that she did not care how
much in earnest anyone became about loving her.
She wanted to be loved until it hurt her.

So she said, "My name is Amaryllis."

The boy studied her a long time.

"That's a funny name for you," he said. "It's a
beautiful name, and if I had known your name was
Amaryllis——"

He took her head very carefully between his hands
and turned it around until she could see the far side
of the garden. And there, on a tall, slender stem,
was a head of lilies bigger than the Madonna lilies,
and red, as red as any red ribbon you ever saw, or
the reddest bird, as red as the blood that seeped if
you let the knife slip and cut your finger playing
"Mumble-ty-peg"—wonderful red velvet flowers
laughing on their stem. John Guido said they were
the only red flowers in the garden; they were so pre-

cious they had to be kept in the cellar in the winter. And their name was amaryllis. She had been named for the red flowers, and John Guido had gone and made her out of the white flowers of the blessed Madonna. Now he would have to go to work and make her all over with an amaryllis lily. He said, too, that the red lily was the flower of love because red was the color of love. He said that, on his violin, when he began to practice, he would play for her a dance of the fairies, the loveliest dance of all dances, which was her minuet because its name was "Amaryllis." When they finished the gorgeous red lady and put her in her glass of water, they went up to the house carrying all of the ladies very carefully and put them on a table in a cool place on the back porch.

Marie came, a French Marie, from the market gardener's on the other side of the fence, and she cooked a fine supper and put it on the table on the porch for them, with the lily ladies for a centerpiece. The flowers were so pretty that Marie talked floods of French nonsense to them as she served the children. She told John Guido to call her when he was ready and she would come and undress his little lady cousin and put her to bed. She would bring her nightie and sleep on the davenport close beside her so if she wanted a drink in the night she would be there to give it to her.

All the world was lovely with the delicate, fragrant loveliness of June, with bloomful old pear trees and cheepy baby orioles, and fat robins, and sweet as honey with red clovers. There was not a thing to bother about, there was not a thing to trouble about because, when she had finished her supper, Amaryllis went and stood beside John Guido's chair. He put an arm around her and she climbed up on the arm to lay her face up against his cheek. Sometimes he slipped his best crusty bite into her mouth and then she put one into his. And because she loved him so, Amaryllis forgot that her mouth might not be clean, so she made his cheek all smeary where she kissed it. But he did not care a bit. He only laughed. When it came to kisses he was a Little Hungry Heart himself.

And when she said, "John Guido, if I stay here as many as three days, by the end of that time, will you love me a teeny bit?"

John Guido laid down his fork. He took his napkin and wiped her mouth carefully, and then he wiped his own mouth.

He said, "Look here, Amaryllis. Down in the brook the very first minute that I saw your yellow head, your taffy molasses head, and your big blue eyes, your cornflower eyes, and your pink cheeks, your wild sweetbriar cheeks, I loved you, and I have been loving you harder every minute ever since, and the thing that's going to almost kill me is going to be the time when your father comes and finds you and takes you away from me."

Amaryllis threw her arms around his neck and hugged him so tight that she could not hug a bit tighter. She gave all she had.

She said, "John Guido, I just love you, and love you, and love you! I love you all I ought to love my father, and I love you all I would love my mother if she wanted me to love her, and I love you all I would love Peter if he wanted me to love him, and I love you all you can ever want me to love you just by yourself alone."

And John Guido said, "No, Amaryllis, you aren't big enough. You don't know enough to love me all I would ever want you to love me, because some of these days you are going to grow as big as I am now, and I am going to grow as big as my father. Some of these days I am going to be a man, taller and broader, and maybe I will look as well as my father but not *like* him—for my father has hair and eyes like yours. But anyway, I will look as well as *I* can, and maybe I can learn to play as well as my mother sang. And by that time you will be a tall lady and your dresses will be way down below your knees and some of them will be all velvet white like the Madonna lilies, and some all fire red like the amaryllis lilies, and some pink and yellow like the roses. Then I will come and I will kneel down before you, and

I will put kisses just on your feet then, and I will say, 'Amaryllis, do you love me yet?' "

Then Amaryllis took both her little hands and plastered them over his mouth and she said, "John Guido, when you get to be a big man and come to me and say, 'Amaryllis, do you love me yet?' I'll say, 'Yes, John Guido, I always have loved you from the minute you came down the creek making the birds sing and the lambs baa-a-a-a and the water laugh— ever since that day, you are the only one I love or that I am ever going to love.' Now come on and play me about how the amaryllis lilies dance."

So John Guido tuned his violin. Very carefully he tuned it. Then he began to play. Something happened that John Guido had not expected. He did not know that there was music in the feet of Amaryllis or that she had been carefully taught to dance. John Guido had no way to know that. Just as soft and easy when he began to make those first singing notes, "Tum, tum—Tum, tum—Tum, tum, tum," Amaryllis's feet began to step right in measure. Her dimpled body began to sway in rhythm. He had not played many measures when away went Amaryllis across the living room, across the back porch, beckoning him to follow, down the back steps, down the footpath, into the old garden where the moonlight was a white sheet, where the pear trees sweetened the night to heavenly fragrance. Down the garden she went until she reached the red lilies. The lilies seemed almost black in the moonlight and the boy with the big black eyes and the lips of reverence, with the long, slender hands of an artist, stood beside the red lilies and played the dainty, exquisite minuet, the most exquisite minuet that ever has been written by any musician. And holding her little yellow skirts, with love to show her how, Amaryllis danced. The moon of that night looked down on as fair a scene in the old magic garden as it ever in all this world had seen anywhere. When she had danced and danced until she was so tired and her little feet were almost skinned, she held up her arms and John Guido lifted her up and carried her back to the house. He went to the side fence and called for Marie.

Marie came and, without asking any questions or interfering with anything that was none of her business, did what she was told to do. She carefully bathed the tired little girl and brushed her hair, and put one of John Guido's old pajamas on her. Then she asked her if she wanted to say her prayers.

Amaryllis did not know any prayer to say. Nobody ever had taught her. Marie thought that was a very wicked thing, a shocking thing for a darling little girl not to know a prayer.

So she said, "Amaryllis, I will teach you the prayer that I say."

Amaryllis sat on the edge of Mr. Forrester's big hand-carved mahogany bed and shook a willful head.

"I'm not going to say your prayer!" she protested. "If I have to say a prayer I'm going to say John Guido's prayer."

The end of that was that Marie went and called John Guido. He was out in the old orchard, but he came to the window and, when Amaryllis raced over to him and put her little hands on his cheeks and said, "John Guido, did your singing mother ever teach you a little night prayer?" John Guido said, "Yes."

Amaryllis smiled at him in the moonlight and said, "Teach it to me, so the good God will love me, too."

John Guido said, "Tonight I'll tell you the first two lines, and tomorrow night I'll tell you the next two, and the next night I'll tell you the last two, because you can't remember them all at once."

Standing before the window, Amaryllis laid her hands together as John Guido showed her, shut her eyes, and repeated after him:

> *Gentle Saviour, at Thy knee,*
> *A little child, looks up to Thee . . .*

Then Amaryllis held up her lips and John Guido leaned over and touched them with another light kiss. From the window sill he picked up both little hands and he kissed them over and over again. And he was not at all particular that those were light kisses. They were kisses of worship, of adoration, kisses of passionate boy love, from the very depth of a heart that had thought itself lonely and hungry and had learned that it did not know the meaning either of loneliness or of hunger since all his life he had been loved and loved abundantly. It was not lack of all love, it was mother love, a little sister's love, that John Guido had missed.

Fifty miles away, in a mansion on the big island, white-faced, breathless people were colliding with each other as they rushed back and forth, because Amaryllis was lost and no one knew where to find her. In the police station a frightened young man sobbed over and over the story of how the child had begged to sit on the stone in the sun for an hour and the sun had been hot and he had fallen asleep, and when he had awakened, the car door was open. She must have come back, because her hat and her purse were lying in the road and there was not a sign anywhere of the kidnappers who had snatched her from the car so quickly she had never made a sound.

At police headquarters in the big city, men by the dozen were being rushed frantically to railroad stations, to steamship piers, to roads leading from the city, and a distracted man was walking the floor at his club cursing himself and cursing the woman who had brought a child into the world and then stoutly and stubbornly refused to be a mother. On each side of him two of his best friends, almost equally distracted, strove to keep pace with him and think for him, to do something, to make some suggestion that might be of avail. One of these friends was a particularly good friend who dared to speak the truth.

So he said, "Now, look here, Paul. I'll grant that half the responsibility for this goes to your wife, but I'll say you've got your share for the other half. After all, you are the kid's father, aren't you?"

Paul Minton stopped in his distracted walk and said, "Yes, I am her father. But the court gave her to her mother. She was in her mother's care. The judge gave the boy to me."

"And you are taking such good care of the boy that you can guarantee that there is no chance of anything happening to him?" asked the friend.

Paul Minton stopped and ran his hands through his hair and stared at the man.

"God, no!" he said. "*I'm* not taking care of him! I am sending the checks for running the establishment that his grandfather's will and the court specified he was to live in. I have no more idea than you have where he is or what he is doing this minute. God knows I've been anything but the kind of father that a man should be when he takes the responsibility of bringing children of his blood, bearing his name, into the world."

"How old was your little girl?" asked one of his friends.

Minton answered: "Just a little over five, if I re-

member rightly, and for the love of God, don't say
was!"

"Is she pretty?" queried the friend.

Paul Minton stopped and tried to remember. Suddenly there danced before him a vision of gold curls
and blue eyes and pink cheeks, and he answered in a
hushed, stricken voice, "God, yes! perfectly beautiful! A perfectly beautiful little thing! I'd say she is
lovely!"

"And I suppose from the clothes she wore, the car
she rode in, with your monogram on the door very
likely, that whatever bandit took her will hold her
for a good stiff ransom."

Minton licked his dry lips.

"How soon could a body reasonably expect an
offer to come?" he asked. "Get the chief of police on
the wire. Tell him it doesn't make any difference
what they ask. Tell him to say that they can have
every damned thing I've got. I'll start over again, if
they bring back the baby safely and give me another
chance."

So the friend went to the telephone and called the
chief of police and told him precisely that.

Morning came lovingly out in the house surrounded by the old orchard, touched into glory the
garden of magic. Amaryllis awoke, and before she
lifted her head from the pillow she remembered
right where she was. She remembered what a good

time yesterday had been, so she sat up on the edge of the bed and called for Marie at the top of her voice. Marie could not have been far away, because she came very quickly, and in no time the child was dressed again in the clothing she had worn yesterday. Then she had her breakfast and was out in the garden ready to play with the marvelous boy again.

There never could have been another such boy in all the world. First they put fresh water into the glasses and a little salt to keep the lady dolls on the back porch in nice shape. Then they chased butterflies and looked through a glass that made their wings big so all the millions of little feathers on them showed. Then they went down to the brook and Amaryllis sat on the bank and fished. She held a long alder shoot with a fine line on it and a bent pin hook with a little worm in the water, and caught one of the shiny fish with silver sides dotted with red paint and speckles on its nose. She shouted with laughter. The sun shone again that day, and the birds sang happier because she was so happy. When she was tired of fishing, they put the little fish back in the water and let it go home, and, hand in hand, they went on down the creek until they were hungry.

By then it was noon, and they went back through the garden for food. After lunch, Amaryllis went to sleep in an old hammock in the back yard. The boy swayed it gently and she slept a long time. When she wakened she had the best orange she had ever tasted. Then she and the boy started out through the meadow to make friends with the sheep and with a cow that lived there, and to see how many different flowers they could find. Sometimes they played Indians, and the boy hid behind the bushes and Amaryllis came down the path, a little happy girl dancing in the sunshine. He jumped out and caught her, looking very fierce and warlike. She was supposed to cry and be afraid. But she was not a bit afraid at being caught by John Guido, because she threw her arms around his neck and hugged him tight every time he caught her. Sometimes she hid in ambush and caught him when he came past, but no matter who was the Indian, or how fierce the capture, the captivity always ended in a kiss.

So they played on until supper time, a whole long, glorious day. Many times they sat down and talked for a long, long time. Amaryllis told the boy about the long, long days at home, and about the chauffeur who kept the dog and the pony, and about the butler who opened the front door like a footman, and about the cook and the governess and the nursemaid and all the people who made up the family that had no mother. The boy grew troubled, and he looked more sober every minute.

He said to her, "Amaryllis, I'm afraid you're awful rich."

Amaryllis said no, she did not think she was. She thought she was very poor. She thought she was a little girl who was left behind the big bronze gates because there was not enough money to take her along when her mother went across the water in a big boat, or else she surely would have taken her. The boy thought about that a while, and he did not know what to think, because he could not quite imagine a mother who could go away and leave such a sweet-smelling, blue-eyed, adorable little thing as Amaryllis.

That night he played again in the garden and Amaryllis danced before the red lilies. Then she went to bed. While Marie undressed her, the boy waited outside the window. When she was all ready to go to sleep in one of his pajamas with the sleeves rolled up and pinned closer at the neck, she came to the window again, and he taught her the next two lines of his prayer.

Keep me safely through starshine,
Make a loving heart of mine . . .

Without a bit of help she remembered the first two lines.

Then Amaryllis went to sleep—went to sleep with the feel of hugs, tight hugs, around her body, and the feel of warm kisses on her lips and on her hair and her cheeks. It was wonderful, more wonderful than anything that ever had happened to her in all the world. It was so wonderful that she was restless in the night and tossed a bit and moaned because she was so afraid that the policeman might come and take her home, as policemen did come and take lost children back to their homes every once in a while.

But it was not the policeman who came about ten o'clock the following morning. It was the boy's father. Walked right in, all unexpectedly. A big, tall man with bright blue eyes and pink cheeks and hair nearly as yellow as the hair on Amaryllis' head. The very minute he saw Amaryllis, and the very minute he heard ten words, he said sternly, "But this will not do at all! There will be people somewhere who are frantic about her. Her mother probably will be half insane."

Amaryllis stood back and shook her yellow head and held on tight to the boy with the black hair and the black eyes.

She stamped her little foot and said, "No! No! Mother doesn't care or she wouldn't go away across the big water and leave me! Father doesn't care or he wouldn't stay at the club all the time and leave me. Nurse Benson and the governess lady are *glad*, because they don't have to work when I'm not there to make them bother."

The painter man whistled softly and then he studied his son intently. Something had happened to the lad since he last looked into his eyes. He had left a child, a little, irresponsible, lonesome-eyed fellow, swallowing hard to keep down a lump in his throat because Father was going away far off on the train, while he was left at home, trying very hard to be brave about it, and not succeeding so very well. He had come back to find the boy so much taller that he scarcely knew him. In his eyes there was a look of maturity, a look of pain, that he could not fathom.

He said, "Oh, boy, oh, John Guido, what is it? What hurt you?"

John Guido answered, "It has been so wonderful to have a little sister. It has been the very sweetest thing, Father."

Then John Guido looked his father straight in the eye and told the first very terrible great big lie that he ever had told in all his life. He told it for Amaryllis.

He said, "I truly don't think anyone wants her, Father. I don't think anyone cares *how* long she stays. We aren't so awfully far from the road. If they had wanted to come and hunt good, they could have found her here. We haven't hidden. We've played out in the garden and around the house all the time. This is three days we've played, and no one has come. I think we can keep her."

His father looked at him very hard and then he said softly, "John Guido, do you *want* to keep this little Amaryllis?"

John Guido never said a word. He just looked back, and the big tears began to gush from his eyes and roll down over his cheeks. The painter man was astounded; also he was a little bit hurt. He thought he had done a better job than that at being both a father and a mother. He did not know that the one thing in all this world that no man can do is to take the place of a mother.

So John Forrester sat down in his big chair and took his son on one knee and Amaryllis on the other, and talked to them a long time. Every word he said was a futile word, useless, to the limit. He found out very thoroughly and clearly for himself that any child who lives alone has lost half its birthright in not having a brother or a sister with whom to play, and if it has had no one, then the disaster is irremediable. He found out that there was something about little Amaryllis that had wakened up something in his boy that had never been there before. Back in the wide, dark eyes there was a steely light he could not budge or combat. Over the full red lips a quiver was running, while, as he watched the boy closely, the father could see the pace at which the heart in his breast was beating. He studied Amaryllis, examined her carefully. The yellow dress was hanging in festoons, and part of the festoons was ruffle and part was lace. It was disgracefully soiled and dirty, but there was nothing anyone could think about Amaryllis except that all her life she had been bathed and brushed and cared for exquisitely.

When he could not force John Guido to admit that it would be the thing for him to do to try to find Amaryllis' father; when Amaryllis set both hands against him and pushed hard and said he was a bad man and she would not like him, and if he sent her back to the big empty house that had no family in it, among the trimmed trees with the shaved grass and the flowers that were not a bit like the meadow and John Guido's garden, that some way she would get out of the gate again, and she would come right straight back, because she was not ever going to live anywhere except in John Guido's garden, and she was not ever going to love anybody except him—John Forrester decided he would be forced to take matters in his own hands. Amaryllis, stoutly refusing to tell the remainder of her name or where she lived, continued her pleading. She was full to the brim and running over with promises to be good and to be obedient. She thought she could help straighten up the rooms. She was willing to do anything except to leave John Guido.

So Mr. John Forrester watched the two children go hand in hand down the back walk, and a great big lump grew in his throat, because the last thing he had heard as they went down the steps was Amaryllis asking anxiously, "John Guido, do you think he will send for the policeman to come and get me today?"

In the sunshine he had seen John Guido kneel down and put his arms around the small girl that might very well have been his little sister and bury his dark face against her neck and he could see the quivering shoulders of his boy. What to do he did not know. By what he was feeling in his heart he knew what it was that he must do. So he went to the telephone and asked for the chief of police of the big city that was not so many miles away.

When he got the chief, he said, "Have you had inquiries for a lost little girl answering to the name of Amaryllis?"

Distinctly he could hear the gasp at the other end of the line. He could hear the panting voice crying, "My God, yes! Do you know anything about the Minton child? Is she safe?"

Mr. Forrester answered, "Put me in touch with her father, please."

It was only a few minutes more until another panting, breathless voice was on the line crying, "Have you got my baby? Have you got my little Amaryllis?"

You would not have thought that even two sleepless nights and three days of torture could have crowded that amount of anguish into the voice of Mr. Paul Minton, club man, gentleman of wealth and leisure.

Mr. Forrester answered, "There is a little girl at my house answering to the name of Amaryllis. She says she ran away from home because her mother crossed the ocean and did not take her along, and because her father and her brother did not want her and no one loves her. If that is the *case*, we are perfectly willing to take care of her where she is."

Then what sounded considerably like incoherent babbling was renewed at the other end of the line, but out of it there seemed to come something that was freighted with certainty that Amaryllis' father *did* love her, and her brother *did* want her, and where were they to come to find the little darling, and would she be safe until they reached her? There was something about taking every care in the world of the child because she was worth millions.

When that came over the line very distinctly to Mr. John Forrester, he laughed. It was a laugh that had something cuttingly sarcastic, something extremely nasty about it. What he said was, "Are you laboring under the impression that there are very many children on this island who are *not* worth millions to the fathers whose blood is in their veins, whose names they bear?"

Just for a minute there was silence at the other end of the line, so Mr. Forrester continued, "Whenever you get ready, come over on the island, take the Meadowbrook Hunt Club road . . ." and there followed minute directions as to which way to turn, and which way to follow Roaring Brook, and exactly where a mail box on the road bearing the name of Mr. John Forrester would indicate the way to a footpath that would lead down a lane and to a little white house where the children were playing in a garden.

Then Mr. John Forrester went to his back door and looked out in the garden and saw two children, not making flower dollies, not playing "Mumble-ty-peg," not chasing butterflies—two children sitting very soberly in a bed of striped grass with their arms tight around each other and their faces laid together, cheek to cheek. Big solemn tears were running down the brown cheeks of the boy and the pink cheeks of the girl.

When he slipped down as near as he could go without being seen, what he heard was, "John Guido, I'm just scared to death for fear your father's gone and told the policeman."

John Guido said not a word, but the tears grew bigger and rolled faster. Mr. John Forrester went back to his studio and got out his paint and his brushes and put on his working blouse and smoked a pipe furiously. He made passes at a canvas in front of him with a brush laden with exquisite paint mixed from half a dozen different colors and wiped it dry and tried again. By and by, he drew his sleeve across his own eyes and said, "Oh, damnation! I don't think there is anything in all this world for me to do except to take the boy and go straight to Italy and start him on his music. Maybe among his mother's people there will be another boy or a little girl related to him who will help him to get over this."

Then he told himself one of the things that grown

people always do tell themselves about children for-
getting and the hurts of childhood being healed, and
rot of the kind, because deep down in his heart he
knew perfectly well that the hurts of childhood never
are healed, and that the one thing above all other
things a child never does is to forget the thing that
really has seared into its little soul deeply enough to
make a scar.

While he was laboring to try to put something
that was in his mind on the canvas, there came a
furious hammering at his door, and he stepped into
the living room with a palette dotted with wet paint
in his left hand and a brush in his right, and stood
looking through the screen at two or three men who
were gathered on the small veranda. From their uni-
forms it was easy to select the policemen of the
group, and from his lack of uniform and a haggard,
red-eyed face, it was easy to select the man with light
hair and blue eyes and a fresh complexion to whom
almost anyone would have awarded Amaryllis for a
daughter.

Mr. John Forrester, because he was nervous and
because he was hurt to the soles of his shoes, took the
paint brush and rolled it in the green paint very
deliberately for a long second. Then he looked at
the door and said in the low, easy voice that charac-
terized a very distinguished gentleman, "Will you
be kind enough to come in?"

But he did not step forward. He did not open the

door. Mr. Paul Minton opened the door for himself and came inside. He looked at the man before him and then he cried, "You telephoned me?"

Mr. John Forrester wiped the paint brush through the green paint with a little more deliberation than before and said with withering precision, "I am the man who telephoned the chief of police the fact that a little lost girl answering to the name of Amaryllis is playing in my garden."

The man with the light hair and the blue eyes cried at him, "Don't you know *who* that child is?"

Mr. John Forrester wiped the brush through the paint and looked through eyes narrowed very nearly to steely slits, "No, I don't know who the child is," he said, "and I don't care the tenth of a damn who she is, or how much money she's worth, or how many relatives neglect her. The only thing I am concerned with is the fact that she says she is five years old, and she says she waited a long time to get the chance to run away because her mother went across the ocean without her, and her father and her brother do not love her. If you are her father and you have arrived at the conclusion that you *do* love her, she is out in my garden. You may go and get her. I'll be damned if I will. All I want you to understand about this is that we had nothing to do with her being here. She climbed from her automobile and ran away by herself, because she preferred to risk what might happen to her among strangers to what she knew would happen to her if she went back home!"

Then Mr. John Forrester turned on his heel, went into his studio, and shut the door behind him with elaborate finality.

Mr. Paul Minton crossed the back porch and started down the path that led to the garden. Glancing down the sunlit way, he saw, standing in the path in front of a bloom-laden white syringa bush, a slender slip of a boy with bare feet, arms bared to the elbows, a rounded throat rising above an open blouse, as handsome a boy, he thought, as he had ever seen. The boy's hands were extended in front of him, and clinging to them stood a little figure with a clean face, with carefully brushed curls, and as soiled and bedraggled a dress as the veriest beggar might have worn. As he stood staring one instant at the picture before him, he saw Amaryllis tugging at the boy's hands. He saw her small face lifted; he heard her plaintive tones: "John Guido, I am *hungry* again! I'm just *hungry* for love, John Guido! Won't you *please* kiss me *again?*"

Mr. Paul Minton stood and stared, and the heart that he had thought had been rather sorely tried for several days began to be tried for sure. He never moved a muscle when the dark-haired boy fell on his knees and put his arms around the little girl and said, "Amaryllis, you will *kill* me! I just *know* that I am going to have to give you up, and I don't think that I can bear it."

Mr. Paul Minton stood still and waited, and by and by, he saw Amaryllis lift herself from the boy's arms and stand up. Very distinctly he heard her ask, "John Guido, if a policeman or my father or the butler comes after me, must I go?"

He saw the shaken body of the boy and heard the agony of his tones as he sobbed, "Yes, Amaryllis. You *belong* to them. You have got to go."

Then he saw Amaryllis stamp her little foot.

"I don't! I don't!" she shrieked. "I don't belong to them! They don't belong to me! They don't *want* me! I belong to you. I belong to you, John Guido, just to you!"

To that the boy said never a word. He stretched out his arms once more, and again he covered the little gold head with kisses, and again it was Amaryllis who stepped back, and again her voice was very distinct.

"John Guido," she said, "if they come to get me, I won't stay with them. I'll run away from them again and I'll come back to you. Every time they get me, I'll come back to you. If they get me a thousand times, some way I'll get away from them, and I'll come back to you. Do you want me, John Guido?"

The dark-haired boy, on his knees on the hard, worn, narrow footpath there in the neglected garden, stretched out his arms. "Want you, Amaryllis?" he said. "Do I want you? Even God up in heaven doesn't know how much I want you!"

Right then Mr. Paul Minton felt the hand of the police lieutenant on his shoulder and knew that there was no more time to be wasted. Business was business. The episode was over. The Minton child had been found. It was time to race back to the city and find someone else's child. So he pushed the rickety gate a little wider open and stepped through.

When he becomes a very old man, with very white hair and shaky hands, he will still remember the horror on the face of little Amaryllis when she looked up and saw him coming down the pathway. He heard the shrill shriek that broke from her lips. He saw her catch the hands of the boy and try to drag him with her as she turned to flee. The boy turned and took one look at him and then threw himself full length in the bed of striped grass, and frantically pulled the long blades together across his ears, so that he could not hear. Alone little Amaryllis headed down the path and darted into the meadow.

It took some fairly speedy running on the part of an agile policeman to run her down and catch her. He was forced to carry her back. As they recrossed the garden with her and carried her around the house and out to the road, until the last faint echo died away, over and over there came her shrill little cry, "Don't you mind, John Guido! I'll come back! I'll come back to you!"

PART THREE

Love, the Alchemist

Love, the Alchemist

By the time the automobile was reached, Amaryllis had learned that, while the touch of the policeman who was carrying her was firm, it was gentle. She had persisted in pressing her face against the glass and screaming, "I'll come back!" at the top of her voice until long after the highway had been reached and she knew no one at the little house could hear her. When they could no longer hear her, she told the world. Some way she reinforced her soul by reiterating her determination. She lay back exhausted on the breast of the policeman, and by and by she discovered that an effort was being made by Mr. Paul Minton to take her into his arms. She was old enough to know that he was her father. She had lively remembrances of at least the better part of four and a half years when she had seen him daily. Sometimes he had picked her up. Sometimes he had

slipped his fingers under her dimpled chin. Sometimes he had put money into her hands concerning
the value of which she knew nothing because she
never had been privileged to spend money herself.
She only knew that it was a thing greatly coveted,
because the nurses and governesses and the housekeeper and the butler were all so eager to relieve her
of it. She knew it was something they wanted very
much.

Her great adventure over, her capture made sure,
swiftly being carried back to the things she loathed,
all the naughtiness and resentment in the heart of
Amaryllis boiled to the surface and, when her father
reached shaking hands and wanted to take her in his
arms, she very promptly made up the horridest face
she knew, embellished with twisty, squinted eyes, a
wrinkled nose, and a wide-opened mouth from
which a little red tongue was thrust just as far as it
would go and waggled in defiance. Because she had
no other refuge, she clung tight to the policeman.
So you can very easily see that between the little
white house on the island and his apartment in the
big city, Mr. Paul Minton had time aplenty to do
considerable thinking. As a matter of fact, he had
already had three days of uninterrupted and agoniz-
ing thinking. He had suddenly discovered that there
was something in blood, that there was something in
parenthood, and however abominably he had failed

in the past, there might at least be hope for the future.

The automobile had made half the journey before Amaryllis straightened her face and leaned her yellow head against the blue coat of the policeman to rest. The blue of the police uniform is particularly attractive as a background for sun-colored curls and deep blue eyes and a delicately flushed pink skin, and from the bottom of his heart Mr. Paul Minton envied that policeman against whom his little girl leaned her head. He would have given a staggeringly large sum to have had her head laid confidingly over his heart. He had thought of practically everything there was to think of concerning his personal affairs during the past three days. He had even thought of going to Europe and taking Amaryllis along and trying to find her mother; of trying to make some sort of plea that would bring her back to her home. But the more he thought of this, the more hopeless he knew it was, because in the twelve years that he had been married to Amaryllis' mother he had learned to the depths the littleness and the selfishness in her soul, and he had very grave doubts as to whether there was any way in which the ingrained vanity, greed, and personal exaltation in which she specialized could be overcome. It would have been the ideal thing to do, but things in this world are seldom ideal. So he laid that idea back on the shelf with the thought that he might better send a personal representative to see exactly where the lady was, and what she was doing, and to learn for sure whether she really was a suitable person to have charge over anything so adorable as Amaryllis.

Exactly when Paul Minton found out that Amaryllis was adorable it would be difficult to say, but one might hazard a guess that he found it out when a dark-haired boy of such extreme beauty that he made a startling apparition, dropped on his knees before her and stretched out his arms to her and cried in a broken voice, "Amaryllis, you will kill me with your sweetness!"

Some way, what he had seen and what he had heard set Paul Minton to studying Amaryllis, to looking at her intently, and what he saw was a little girl, sane and normal, beautifully developed, beautiful of face and hands and body, and spoiled to the last degree it was possible to spoil a child. Even when she had wrinkled up her nose and stuck out her tongue and made herself as ugly as ever she could, she had been adorable, and, looking at her, he had not wanted anything in all the world quite so much as he wanted to cover her little face and her hands and her bare dimpled feet even with kisses straight from his heart.

And she preferred a policeman to him! Children habitually, as he had known them, had been frightened of policemen. They had been taught that "a policeman would get them" and do something particularly distressful to them, and so it was all the more to be wondered at that Amaryllis preferred the policeman to her father.

He tried to figure it out. He could not remember that he had ever struck the child. He could not remember that he had ever spoken harshly to her or brushed her out of his way. He tried to think deeply, but he had not the knowledge that would have furnished him the motive for thinking deeply enough to realize that no child resents being punished if it knows that it has been naughty and deserves punishment. The blows that children resent are the blows of anger, of injustice, of intimidation, of hate. No child resents being corrected if it is thoroughly convinced that it deserves correction, if it may rest afterward on a breast that it fully understands is its loving refuge, if there are kisses and consolation and promises of help to make the future better. But having had no experience, Paul Minton could not possibly know these things.

The first thing that arrested the attention of Amaryllis was when her father leaned forward with instructions to the chauffeur. They were to be taken to Mr. Minton's apartment in the city. Amaryllis' eyes widened suddenly. She began to think. She began to study Paul Minton. Then she discovered the most astounding fact that ever had penetrated her young consciousness: he had been crying. His eyes were all swollen and red and his cheeks were tear smeary, exactly like hers had been many a time when she faced herself in the mirror and talked to the little person there because she had no one else to talk to. Slowly Amaryllis' eyes widened; slowly her mouth fell open. The powerful big man, the handsome man, the beautifully dressed man, the man with the ready laughter on his lips, the man for whom everyone stood aside, whom all the servants about the house feared to displease, the man who earned the money to make things happen in the big city, the man who had never taken her where he lived, was crying! Suddenly she leaned toward him.

"Where am I going?" she asked.

"You are going with me," answered Paul Minton sternly.

Amaryllis' mouth halfway closed. She thought some more. She was not perfectly sure whether it would not be as bad to go with him as it would to go back to Benson and the housekeeper and the cook. At least she could throw things at them, and she was not sure she would dare throw anything at him and, besides, she had gotten away from them once, and what one has done once, there is every possibility that one may do again. Even a little girl of five years knew that. And if running away the first time had been so perfectly delightful, why could she not run away a second time? Five years was old enough to figure out that maybe running away the second time might not be exactly like the first. She might not find the right road. She might not find the black-eyed boy. He had said that the marsh she had passed was almost bottomless in places, and if she had tried to cross it and had gotten in it, she would have gone down in the black muck to stay. So maybe running away would not be so wonderful unless she could find her way back to the brook that roared and the boy who copied his music from the birds and made the flowers sing. If she should find the wrong kind of a boy and he should beat her and abuse her, that would not be so very good. What she would have to do would be to wait until she was big enough to manage it and then, in some way, surely she would find the roaring brook and the little white house again. So very definitely Amaryllis settled it in her mind that she would run away whenever she got the chance. But there was only one place in all the world to which she wanted to run—straight to the roaring brook, straight to the beautiful meadow, back to the grow-as-you-please garden with the striped grass and the flaming red lily that was her lily, back to the sympathetic boy whose touch was so gentle, whose lips were so comforting, whose fingers were full of magic, and whose heart was so full of tenderness, and from whose thoughts came music so wonderful that the very birds stopped their singing and came closer to hear how music should be made. She wondered, if her father kept her long in the big city, what her chances would be of running away from there. She decided they would not be nearly so good as they would be in the big house where she lived alone with people who were paid to take care of her.

After she had thought a very long time, Amaryllis looked at her father again and, with this thought in the back of her head, she told him what she had heard the servants say.

"I don't belong to you; I belong to Mother."

Mr. Paul Minton answered in a voice that she did not know, a voice she never before had heard. He said,

"Yes, darling, I know that. But I am going to see the judge who made that decision, and I am going to get it revoked, and after this you are going to belong to me."

Again Amaryllis was not sure that she wanted to belong to him. She thought about it quite a while. Peter belonged to him, and Peter was as miserable as she. She played with a button on the nice policeman's coat and then she said, "Do you want me to belong to you now?"

And Paul Minton said, "Yes, Amaryllis. I want you now."

Amaryllis could not understand that. She thought quite a while. She looked at the swollen red eyes and the lined face and the shaking hands, and then she said very deliberately,

"Did you find out you wanted me because I ran away?"

"Yes," said Paul Minton, "I found out that you were my very own little girl, that the blood in your veins is of my blood, that your hair is like mine, and your eyes are like mine, and as much as a little pink and white girl can be like a big man you are like me. The first time we come to a mirror I will hold you up and let you see how much you are like me."

"I wish," said Amaryllis, "that instead of finding out that you wanted me, you had found out that you *loved* me."

Then Amaryllis closed her lips and drew back against the coat of the policeman and stared straight at her father through narrowed eyes. She did not know why the big tears began rolling down his cheeks. She did not know why his hands were shaking. She did not know why no words came when he opened his mouth and his lips moved. Finally he got it said,

"But that's exactly what I did find out, Amaryllis. If I hadn't found out that I loved you, I wouldn't want you; I would just think you were a bother and a nuisance and something to interfere with my pleasure, and I don't think that now, at all. I think you are the nicest little girl that I ever knew, and I think that I will never let you out of my sight again unless you are with somebody I know I can trust absolutely. I think that if I try very hard to behave as a good father should, maybe some day you will not make faces at me and you will not rather sit on a policeman's lap than on mine."

Amaryllis sat very still, and she looked at her father very hard. Then she looked up at the policeman. She discovered something. The policeman was pushing her. The hands that had been holding her, the lap on which she sat, every bit of that policeman's body was very gently shoving her toward her father. Amaryllis was not in any hurry. She had been a little Hungry Heart too long. The agony of loneliness and neglect had bitten too deep. She could not get over it all in a minute, but she did know how to be polite. She did not like to see a big man cry, no matter how much she cried, and the policeman was still urging her in the direction he supposed she should go. So suddenly she lifted both hands toward Paul Minton and without the least enthusiasm she said,

"All right, then, if you are really sure that you love me now, I'll sit on your lap."

The transfer was made and, while there was no wild enthusiasm about it, it was at least a transfer. Paul Minton at last had his baby on his lap, in his arms where he could stroke her silky hair and find out for himself the wonder of dimpled little hands and tapered fingers and chubby feet that were rather badly scratched and scarred from their three days of running bare.

"Where are your shoes?" he asked.

Amaryllis laughed, and suddenly she began to talk, and Paul Minton learned all about the brook

that roared and the little speckly fish in it and the
flowers on the banks and the birds that sang over it
and the joy of having bare feet in running water. He
learned that his little daughter had not the slightest
idea of the value of property, because she answered
casually: "Oh, I just threw them away because I
didn't want to bother with them."

He remembered that he had thrown a good many
things away because he did not want to "bother with
them" and they might have been things that somebody else would have been very glad indeed to
"bother" with. So he stored that thought on the shelf
to wait for a future day. That began the practice of
storing things away to wait for future days and, by
and by, he had quite a shelf full of things laid back
that he was going to think about and to work out.

By that time they had reached the apartment
where he lived. Amaryllis shook hands with all the
policemen and said good-by to them very nicely.
She convulsed the biggest policeman, the one whom
all the rest obeyed, when she told him very gravely,

"The next time I run away you needn't bother to
come to find me, because I'll be back at the roaring
brook and with the nice boy, and I will be all right
there. I will be happier than I would any place else
in this whole big world."

Paul Minton put that on the shelf along with the
rest of his collection, and he was not particularly
pleased that anything so attractive as his little daugh-

ter should prefer a strange boy, who had a distinctly disagreeable father, to him. So, from the crossing of the sidewalk into the elevator and up to his rooms, straightway he began to try to think like a little girl. He began to try and find out what a little girl would want. He had to talk to Amaryllis a great deal to learn and he found her point of view was rather a staggering one on many subjects. But before that night, he knew what it was that he had to do.

It sounded simple. Amaryllis wanted a home with love in it. She wanted her dog and her pony. She would like a house where the grass grew long, and she would like the flowers to grow as they pleased, but the principal thing that Amaryllis wanted was somebody who would take care of her because they loved her. She did not want anybody in her house who came there because they were paid money to come. She wanted the big man that opened the front door for her to open it because he loved to let her in. She wanted the nurse who bathed her and dressed her to do it because she loved her and wanted her to be clean. She wanted that same kind of a governess and a chauffeur. She even wanted the cook to love her.

When she was ready to go to bed, she suddenly stopped putting on the things that her father had provided for her and said to him accusingly,

"Now look what you've gone and done! I can't be a good girl and I can't go to heaven when I die unless I say my prayers every night, and the nice boy was teaching me his prayer, and it's not all finished. There are tonight's lines which I don't know yet. Now look what you've gone and done, getting me when I was all nice and happy and learning to say my prayers like a good girl where I was! Nobody ever taught me prayers. They only tucked me in!"

Paul Minton thought away back in his memory and conjured up a vision of a mother who had taught him to kneel down each night and fold his hands, and what was it he had said? He could not remember a thing except "If I should die before I wake," and looking down at the sunshine and rose leaves and blue sky that was Amaryllis, he could not tell her to say that. He never in all his life had felt quite so helpless, quite so small, quite so disgusted with life as he had lived it. So he came to confession.

"Amaryllis," he said, "I haven't been living right. I haven't been doing what I should. It has been so long, I cannot remember the prayer I would like to teach you. You say over what the boy taught you and I will find somebody that's expert on praying, and maybe they can tell me what the lines you lost are. Maybe I can get them for you."

Amaryllis answered very promptly.

"I don't mind so much about the prayer, but I would like best in all the world to have you get the boy for me."

Then she asked suddenly, "Where's Peter?"

And her father answered, "At home, I suppose."

Amaryllis thought that over, and then she said,

"Does Peter have to be lost before you can find out whether you love him or not?"

And Paul Minton answered,

"No, Peter is a nice little man. I've found out about him at the same time that I found out about you, and when I see the judge about you I am going to see him about Peter, too, and after this you and Peter and I are going to live together. We will close up or rent Peter's house and you will both come to a house of mine. I don't know just how we are going to fix it, but I know that it is going to be a nice house and its name is going to be the House of Love. Somewhere I am going to find the people who will take care of you because they love you. It will not be easy, and I may have to try several times, but if you will promise to be a good girl and help me all you can and not run away any more, we will find those people with love in their hearts, and we will find a place to develop love where there is running water and the flowers grow wild and the grass grows long and there are ponies to ride and other children can come to play with you. You shall have everything you need to make you into a real, for-sure little girl, the very finest kind of a little girl that there is anywhere."

Amaryllis thought about that for some time.

"Will Peter *want* to come and live with us?" she asked.

"Yes," said Paul Minton, "when I go to Peter and get down on my knees, and with real tears of sorrow in my eyes tell him how bad I have been and how

sorry I am and how much I love him, Peter will forgive me and he will come and live in our house with
us."

Amaryllis was a thoughtful person. She thought
that over, and then she said gently,

"That will be nice. I always kind of liked Peter.
He tells the truth and he isn't a cad. He's just lonesome and hurt like I was. I kind of like Peter, and
if you are going to find the folks that will take care
of us because they love us, and if we are going to
have a house with love in it, why, I guess maybe I'll
love you, too."

Amaryllis put up her arms and lifted her lips for
the first real kiss she had ever had from her father.

Mr. Paul Minton astonished all his friends and all
his business associates by doing exactly what he had
told Amaryllis he would do. He forgot all about himself and the things he had considered pleasures. He
swallowed his pride and wrote a polite note to Mr.
John Forrester, thanking him for taking care of Amaryllis and for sending for him, and asking if he
might very kindly be supplied with the closing lines
of the little prayer that his son had begun to teach
his little daughter. A few nights later, when Amaryllis folded her hands and said,

> *Gentle Saviour, at Thy knee*
> *A little child looks up to Thee.*
> *Keep me safely through starshine*
> *Make a loving heart of mine . . .*

and then looked reproachfully at her father, he said very gently, "John Guido says to tell you that the rest of it is:

When you want me for your own
Guide my footsteps to your throne!

"Did you see him?" cried Amaryllis.

"No," said Paul Minton, "I did not. I wrote a letter to his father and he told me."

"Is that all he told you?" asked Amaryllis.

"Yes," said her father, "it is."

Amaryllis sighed. "I wish he had told you if he loves me yet," she said.

"Well, he does," said Paul Minton.

"How do you know?" asked Amaryllis.

"Because he is the kind of a boy who would," said her father.

"Then I'll say the prayer," said Amaryllis, "because it's a beautiful prayer and I love it and I love you for getting the rest of it."

She gave him a tight hug and a kiss, and so he had his reward.

Paul Minton did not wait long to see the judge who had used the big knife on his family. He asked for control of his children. He secured a reversion of the former decision. He put tenants in both of the big houses and prepared a house entirely different to live in. There were running water and long grass and singing birds and, though it took a long time and it took considerable money, he succeeded in finding people who were loving and sympathetic, who were honest and careful, who would cooperate with him in rearing his children as all children should be reared. He stuck to the job with unswerving interest. He never went hunting or fishing or polo playing or yachting halfway round the world, or any of all those things that he had used to do, until he had made his children thoroughly happy and they were willing for him to go, until he was very sure that he left them where they would be safe and properly cared for. His reformation was not a thing of a minute. It was an everyday affair that stayed right on the job; and day in and day out, as the years kept coming, Paul Minton kept finding out more things about the heart of a boy and the heart of a girl, and incidentally he learned a number of things about his own heart.

One day, when word came that the children's mother had married a French count and was going to live the rest of her life in France and be a countess, none of them was sorry. They were getting along very well without her. They had learned to mean so much to each other that they really did not need her. Down in his heart Paul Minton hoped that he could be so very loving and tender with Amaryllis, that he could so surround her with things all children are supposed to love, that it would be easy to mold her to his will on all subjects. He had learned through the years, as they went whirling by, that there was one subject upon which he not only could not mold her but could not even touch her. Whenever he reached the subject of the black-haired boy, whenever John Guido came into the foreground, everything else dropped back and stood still, and Amaryllis stood up with wide round eyes and looked her father straight in the face and told him without any reservations,

"I'll go back the very minute I am big enough. I'll go back to the roaring brook and the meadow of the flowers, to the old magic garden and to the boy who makes the music."

It took him several years to find out that every time Amaryllis went driving she drove on the island, and every time she came near running water, she stopped the car and examined it intently. He had let five years pass before he got it through his consciousness that almost every hour of the day, underneath the gaiety of Amaryllis' laughter, deeper than the games she played, deeper than the lessons she studied, deeper than the music and the dancing lessons she insisted on having, there ran an undercurrent.

One day he said to her, "Amaryllis, didn't you used to be rather a naughty little girl?"

Amaryllis thought as long as she always did before she spoke and then, as always was her custom, she told the truth.

"I used," she said, "to be just what I told the black-eyed boy I was. I got it out of a fairy book. I told him I was a little Hungry Heart, and I *was* hungry. I was starved so near to death that it made me cross and fretful, and I was so lonesome that I screamed just to hear the sound of my own voice. Now you have given me love and you have taken away the lonesomeness, and I am trying to be a good girl as you want me to be. I am trying to be so good that when I find John Guido, as I am going to find him some day, he will think that I am nice as his beautiful mother was. I could not ever play music the way he does, but I am going to study hard so I will know about the music he plays. I couldn't ever dance as some people do, but I can dance in the moonlight before the Amaryllis flowers enough to suit John Guido."

Paul Minton thought about that. He thought about it a long time, and one day he called Amaryllis into the library of the big new house and swung her up to the table in front of him and drew up his chair and put his arms around her and looked into her face.

"Amaryllis," he said, "are you still hunting John Guido?"

Amaryllis looked at him and after she had thought it over she reached her decision.

"Yes," she said, "until I am an old lady with white hair and a lace cap and all wobbly on a cane, I will be hunting John Guido—if I don't ever find him before."

Her father said, "Amaryllis, can you tell me what it is that makes you think so much of John Guido?"

And Amaryllis answered for once in her life promptly without taking time to think a minute.

"Sure I can," she said. "He was the first person in all this world who ever loved me. And he did love me. And he loves me yet. He is smiling and he is trying just as hard to be nice for me as I am trying to be nice for him. He is playing my dance, and when it comes the time for me to do it again for him, he will play it more beautifully than even the man who wrote it could play it. When I find him there will not be any other girl he has ever played that dance for, and there will not be any other girl he has put his arms around and whose lips he has kissed, because he promised me and I promised him. I belong to John Guido and he belongs to me."

It was Paul Minton's turn to think. He had done considerable thinking. Now he did some more.

But in the end he said, "Amaryllis, what you have said is a very queer thing and it is an unusual thing, but I can see maybe how it happens that it is a true thing. Now I am going to tell you something. I haven't been such a bad old father as I might have been. I went back and hunted up your John Guido as soon as I got you taken care of. His father is not easy to get along with, and so I did not try to get along with him. I just kept myself in the background where nobody knew anything about me, and through his lawyers and his bankers I put across what I wanted to do. It wasn't very many months after you ran away until John Guido's father took him and went to Italy to live for a long time, for such a long time that he is going to stay there until all that Italy and all that Germany and all that France and England maybe can teach him about the violin has been learned. But I think they intend to come back, because they kept the house and the French girl next door keeps it swept and dusted. But the garden's running to ruin and the house is falling down and lessons cost a lot of money and pictures are not so easy to sell in Italy as they are in this country. So I am going to ask you today if you want me to have the lawyer write to John Guido and his father and ask them if, for the rest of the time that they are staying abroad, they would lease their house to a tenant who wants to fix the roof so that it won't leak, and straighten it up a little, and live in it until they are ready to come back and take it. If they were offered very good terms, it would help to pay their expenses there, and it might give you something that you could do that would give you great pleasure without having a secret in your heart from your old father. You wouldn't need to sneak out in the car and go hunting up every brook on this island, trying to find your own particular brook, if Father took you to it. You would not need to go on hunting the little house and the garden with the red lilies all frozen. You could go to it as you pleased. I could find a discerning man who could take out the weeds and plant more flowers, and it would not hurt to put another hinge on the gate or to make a new gate like it, and to floor the veranda and patch the roof. You might do anything you pleased there, and do it when your dad knows where you are and what you are doing. How would that suit you?"

Amaryllis buried her face down in her father's shirt front and cried until she could not cry any longer, and when she lifted it up she put her arms around his neck, and she laid her soft red lips on his, and for the first time in all her life she said,

"Father, I love you next to John Guido. I love you better than anything except him in all the whole world, and I love Peter, too, because Peter is a nice boy. Father, will you do this and not tell Peter? Not tell anybody? Will you let it be my secret, all mine alone?"

Paul Minton said, "Yes, Amaryllis, I'll do it and it shall be your secret all alone. You may go when you please. You may do what you please over there. I will send workmen and you can tell them what you want done. I will send you an architect to show the workmen how to restore everything and make it strong and secure so it will last until they come back, but leave everything very much as it is so that it will not be a strange or an unfamiliar place."

Amaryllis thought that over for a time and then she asked softly, "Father, could you buy a picture once in a while?"

Paul Minton laughed.

"Amaryllis," he said, "I've given away Forrester pictures until I haven't got a friend who has not one somewhere in his house. There is this to say about them. They are damn good paintings. I don't know a landscape artist in this country, or in Europe either, of the present day who can beat him. He hasn't got a nice temper and he hasn't a very nice manner but he can paint!"

Then Amaryllis said something else, and what she said was this, "Father, Mr. Forrester has had a long time to think things over. Maybe he is nicer now than he was. Just look what a difference there is in *you*. He couldn't know you now without thinking you are a lot nicer than you used to be."

Paul Minton laughed and said: "Yes, Amaryllis, I guess that is the truth. I think you have worked love's alchemy on me as well as you have on John Guido and his father."

After that there was not any way for Amaryllis to be half so nice a girl as she wanted to be. Because her heart was so very full of love and so very full of high hopes and so very full of youth, she made something entirely different out of Peter, just as she had made something entirely different out of her father. Peter did not turn his back and look from the window any more when she talked to him. He came over and sat on her chair arm and put his arm across her shoulder and pulled her ear and there was nothing he liked in the world much better than he liked to kiss her good night and good morning and bring all the boys he knew to see what a nice sister he had. They had fine times riding their horses and playing all sorts of games and swimming and fishing and going in boats.

Religiously Amaryllis tried to think for her father and to think for Peter. She tried to take the place that her mother should have filled in the house. When she had done everything she could think of to do for her family, then she was free to slip to the telephone and call the architect who served her and tell him something more she had thought about that she wanted done to the little house. She kept on thinking of things every time she went there, until by and by, along about the time that there was talk of taking her abroad for the first time, a very wonderful thing happened to the little house and the thirty acres of extremely valuable land that surrounded it. The house itself had been repaired and bolstered up and helped out until it was practically splinter new so far as being upstanding and reliable was concerned. It had shiny waxed floors. It had beautiful woodwork. It had softly tinted walls. It had the same furnishings that always had been in it, and here and there new and different pieces crept in. One thing. had happened that was entirely different. On the right corner in the right light there had grown up the most wonderful studio for a painter that three of the greatest architects in the big city could think up. The plans that all of them made for what they would like to have if they had the money for it were taken and shaken together and made into a studio for a painter that had every single thing in it, every comfort and convenience and quirk of lighting that could possibly be designed. That was for John Forrester.

Over at another side there crept on another room that had not been in the little house before, and that room was the loveliest room that Amaryllis could think up with some very able assistance from people who knew about the kinds of rooms that musicians liked. It was a room with walls of the softest, most delicate green, like spring coming to the willows and the apple trees; a room with woodwork stained the softest gray. The grain of the wood showed through. Soft rugs of gray with a little bit of green, and beautiful chairs and tables and a great piano, a perfect piano, waited for John Guido.

Outside of the house every flower that lifted its head was left, but the weeds were taken away from around them, and some rich soil was offered to them, and pipes ran underground to different places, and water was provided that there need not be any long spells of summer thirst. The fence was straightened up around the little garden, and every weed went out of it never to return. One other thing happened after all the weeds had been taken away, and every tree had had all the dead wood cut from it and all its cavities filled, and there was not a thing left that possibly could be done to make that thirty acres more beautiful than it was—the very last thing of all that love could suggest to the heart of Amaryllis was an order that came from a lily field in the South. Nobody except Amaryllis herself knew how many, because nobody ever went around to count them. But just inside the gate on either hand, quite as if they had stuck up their heads through the long grasses because they loved to, there mysteriously sprang up a great bed of red amaryllis. Down the flower-bordered walk, here and there, one peeped over verbenas and through snapdragons and larkspur and candytuft, and beside the front door they flamed up brilliantly, and all the way around the house and here and there through the orchard. The garden was a flame of them. Of course, they had to be housed in winter and reset in the spring, but no one cared.

There was one thing more that happened in the garden. Only one thing that was any different. Where the one red amaryllis had been set, a space perhaps the size of a large room was cleared. Away down deep it began with cement and crushed rock foundation, and came up a little above the surface and ended with a paving of white marble. A wall ran up at the back the length of it that gleamed white in the moonlight, white as the shimmeriest star high up in the heavens, and a great big urn, of white marble, all carved with doves and cupids racing with garlands and flying ribbons, and fawns running away from the cupids, crowned the center. And in this wonderful urn big bulbs of red amaryllis were set each spring and fertilized, watered, and tended until they lifted up great heads of red velvet lily flowers.

Sometimes, on moonlight nights when nobody in all the house could find Amaryllis, if they had gone to the little garden beside the roaring brook, they would have found her on this marble floor all in a soft white dress—plain and simple, not much of a dress, chiffons that lifted and floated and carried on the night air, white as the whitest ray of moonlight. They would have found Amaryllis with her yellow hair unbound and her blue eyes on either the lilies or the stars. No one could have watched her long without knowing that what she was dancing as she tiptoed and whirled and floated over the marble floor was just "Amaryllis," "Amaryllis," as the big black-eyed boy had played it.

Once Paul Minton got started at being the kind of a father that every man was intended to be, he resorted to no halfway measures. Whether a man lives in a big house with millions at his command, or in a log cabin on potatoes he has raised, milk from his cows, and eggs from his chickens, really being a father is the same kind of a job with every man wherever in this world he may happen to be—just in his own chimney corner doing the level best the strength he has developed and the brain the Lord has endowed him with make it possible for him to do— that is the real kind of a father that every man should be. There is not a doubt at all but that the humblest man who is a father can be a very wonderful kind of a father if he starts by having the love of God in his heart and the love of little children in his heart and the love of his country in his heart. Any man can be the kind of a father Paul Minton was so far as love goes and, after all, it is love that people really want in this world. All her life Amaryllis had had the millions, and they did not matter the least bit. What Amaryllis wanted was love.

So, because there was this great love in her heart, so great that it swayed the heart of her father, letters were written across the sea telling how land values were increasing. When a confidential agent made a report to Paul Minton of how John Forrester and his son were making ends meet in Rome, whenever there seemed to be a stringency, whenever the lessons were unusually expensive or clothing was needed, or a better apartment in a warmer, sunnier place became necessary, mysteriously some rich man

away in the West paid a handsome price for a picture, or a new tenant in the little house on the big
island offered a higher rental. Some way it happened
so that there was always money for a bright, warm
apartment and nourishing food and comfortable
clothing. There were always materials for John Forrester to paint pictures with, always the money to
pay for the lessons for John Guido.

When she could not think of another thing to do
to the little house, Amaryllis slipped into the library
and sat on the table in the position in which her father sometimes placed her, and waited for him.
When he came, he recognized that position and he
laughed as he put his hand in his pocket and asked,

"How much is it this time, Amaryllis?"

Amaryllis said, "Father, it's a lot this time. Do you
think you can leave for a few months?"

Father said yes, he thought he could.

And Amaryllis said, "You know you said it was
time Peter went to Germany and had some of his
lessons there and some of them in England and some
of them in France, and, Father, it is time for me to
go to Italy."

Then Father straightened up suddenly and did
not know exactly what to think.

Before he had time to say anything, Amaryllis explained. "You know, Father, I can't stand it a day
longer unless you promise me that very soon now I
may see John Guido. I won't touch him and I won't

speak to him. I won't even let him know I am there.
I must not interfere with his music. He wouldn't
like it and his father would not like it. But you
know, Father, there is lots of Rome. There would be
a little apartment somewhere across from his where,
through a window, I could look at him. I could just
see if he is growing taller and if his hair has stayed so
black. I could follow, all covered up, in the distance
and watch whether, as he went about his work, he
would see if an amaryllis was growing anywhere.
I could listen to hear whether he plays my minuet
or not. I will give you my word of honor, Father, I
will play the game square. I won't let him see me.
I won't speak to him. I won't do more than maybe
lay my finger on his coat sleeve in a crowd. I won't
even touch him if you say not. But don't you think,
Father, you could only let me see him?"

Paul Minton put his arms around Amaryllis
tightly.

"Get your things ready," he said gruffly. "Tell
Peter to get ready. We will go for as long as you want
to stay. We will go, and in some way it shall be fixed.
I think you are wise in saying that you must not meet
him now. You must not take his mind from his work,
but there will be some way to find out whether he
is thinking about you, whether his heart is the kind
of a heart that is in your breast and, if it is, then you
will be comforted, then you will be ready to come
home and wait until he finishes, won't you, Amaryllis?"

Amaryllis said she would.

So it was not very long until, straight across the
street from the small apartment where John Guido
and his father made music and painted pictures, it
was not so very long until mysterious neighbors that
no one ever saw by daylight moved in, people who
came and went, heavily muffled and clothed, in a
closed car. They did not really live there. They
rented that apartment and, when lessons were
learned and lots of Italy had been seen, when her
heart could not stand it any longer, then Amaryllis,
from a window straight across a narrow Roman
street, watched and waited for John Guido.

The first time he came down the stairway and out
on the sidewalk only one story below her, so close
that she could have reached across and almost whispered a sentence that he would have heard, so close
that she had to clench her fists and hold very tight,
she had to put her hand over her mouth and hold
it shut to keep from calling,

"Guido! John Guido, I am here! It is Amaryllis!"

She thought she could not endure it. At first her
heart ached so badly she thought she could not ever
keep her word. She thought she surely would be
forced to call and say she was sorry afterward. Then
something that had been bred in the years of loneliness and repression stood her in good stead, and she
knew that she could bear it. She knew that she must
watch him and not call. She knew that it would be
selfishness for her to do it, because she knew that he

would come. The reason she knew it was because the John Guido who stood on the sidewalk and looked up and down the street for the man to come with the paper or maybe the milk, that John Guido was her boy.

He had grown, oh, so tall! His hair was even blacker, glossy like silk, and his eyes were so big and wide, and such clean eyes. She could see his long, slender hands. And oh, how happy she was to see that he was comfortably clothed, to see that there were good shoes on his feet, that he looked like the gentleman he was born to be in his attire as well as his person! After she had watched long enough, a shrinking and a timidity grew in her soul. She had not thought that he would be quite so big. She had not realized that there would be a wave of red in his cheeks, the velvet red on his lips. She had not known that youth could look as John Guido looked standing there in the warm Italian sunlight.

Then came days when she followed him. She hired her courier to spy out his hours, how much time he practiced and where he went for his recreation, how he filled in his days. She learned where she might go so that, with bent head and veiled, she might brush by him on the street so close that her garments would touch him.

There was one day when for a few minutes she thought she could not possibly hold out. She had followed him for blocks down a street, and then he

came to an open flower garden, a market under the
sky. He had looked everywhere and had not seen
what he wanted. Then a woman, swarthy and dark,
came hurrying up to him gesticulating and pointing,
and John Guido followed her. Screened and carefully taken care of, she had held up to him a terra-
cotta jar filled with blood-red amaryllis. He had
buried his face in the lilies, and standing there in
the open market, he had kissed their velvet petals.

All the timidity slipped from the soul of Amaryllis, for she knew, just as she knew that the sky was
blue and the stars were holding their places and the
sun and moon were going in their courses, so she
knew that John Guido was keeping the faith, that he
loved her, that she was the thought that every minute
was in the back of his heart, just as he was the
thought that every minute was in the back of hers.
She knew that the old woman was accustomed to
furnishing him red lilies. She had many times before.
She would again.

That night she went straight to the room across
the narrow street and waited and listened. And that
night the violin played "Amaryllis"—played it until
the tears rolled down her cheeks. All alone, with the
driver waiting in the street below, she danced and
danced until she could see the tall form of the elder
Forrester take the violin from the fingers of the boy
and motion him toward his room. He must be in
good shape for his lessons on the morrow.

Then Amaryllis climbed in her car and went back to the hotel where she lived. That night she held counsel with her best friend. She told what she had seen and what she had done and she said,

"Father, I am ready to go home now. I am perfectly satisfied. I know that John Guido loves me and that he is working for me, and that he is waiting for me. God has not made any other girl that can touch him. He is all mine and he will wait for me and I am ready to go."

"All right," said Paul Minton. "Whatever you say. This is your picnic. Shall we go on to Paris and touch up on your French a bit there, and shall we see how the English are living while we are at it?"

"Yes," said Amaryllis, "I am ready to go. But, Father, can I leave, can I go without doing something that will let him know I have been here, that will let him know I am waiting?"

"Let's think about that," said Paul Minton. "I hardly know what to say."

"If you could know," said Amaryllis, "if you could know the joy that is in my heart only to see him, only to see how wonderful he is, to hear him play, to follow him to the market place and to the cathedral, barely to touch him on the streets! I have followed him by the hour, Father, and I have learned that he is all mine. I have seen the prettiest girls in Rome smile at him. I have seen the prettiest girls touring from America and England look at him on the streets—and he doesn't pay any attention. Father, he is waiting, he is waiting for me! He is waiting just for me! And by the joy that is in my heart, knowing that he is waiting, would not it comfort his heart to know that I am waiting? Isn't there some way to work a breath of heart ease for him?"

Paul Minton thought deeply and then he said, "What is it you have in mind? What is it you want to do?"

Amaryllis answered, "I don't know, Father. I haven't got it thought out, but I made you a promise and I am going to keep it. If any way happens that I could let him know that I have been somewhere near, if any way happens, have I your permission?"

Paul Minton kissed his girl and said, "Amaryllis, I think I know what John Guido meant when years ago he said you were so sweet that he thought you would kill him. Sometimes you are so sweet that I think you will kill me! It *would* kill me to have sorrow or trouble or shame come to you. You go on and do what your heart tells you, and your father is going to be reasonably certain that what you do will be what the nicest girl in all the world would do."

It was perhaps three days later that Amaryllis came racing into her father's room in the hotel in Rome and flew into his arms.

"Father!" she cried. "Father! I've got it! Oh, Father, what do you think? Tonight, this very night, he is going to play! He is going to play in a great concert, and away back in a corner somewhere we can slip in and we can hear him and we can see what people will do, and when his last number is played, by an usher I can send him up a red lily, and then we will slip out quickly and we will go straight to our train, and we will not leave any word where we are going or any way that he can find us. We will just let him know that I was there, that I heard him playing, that I am waiting."

All that afternoon Amaryllis wrote notes. She wrote them by the dozen. She filled the waste basket with fragments of them, and when night came and she was dressed more carefully than she ever had been dressed before, dressed with exquisite precision and taste to listen to his music, they found a secluded place in the great building, and with Amaryllis clinging tight to her father's hands, they listened breathlessly. They watched through glasses with straining eyes. They listened to the salvos of applause when, slender and handsome, gracefully and with exquisite skill, John Guido stood before a great audience and played great music.

Then a thing happened that was so surprising that Paul Minton took Amaryllis in his arms and held her tight without the slightest regard as to whether anybody saw what he was doing. Nobody was looking at them anyway. Everyone was looking at the handsome youth playing, playing exquisite music. The program said that it was his first public appearance.

When he had played the great things and the fine
things, and when he had answered encore after encore, at the very last he stood out, and he waited for
a moment as if he could not quite decide. Then he
lifted his violin. He lifted his bow. He shook back
his hair and laughed until the gleam of his white
teeth could be seen across the great building, and
lightly, like thistledown and fairy footsteps, lightly
like Jack Frost coming in the night to paint the
windows with pictures, Tap-tap-tap-tap—the bow
fell and John Guido began to play "Amaryllis."

That was when Amaryllis's old dad had to hold
her tight. Afterward he sent the usher up the aisle
with a great bunch of red amaryllis, and down in the
heart of it there was a little note that said:

*I have heard you play my music. Now I must go
back and leave you to finish your work, but when
you come to the little white house that's waiting for
you, as I promised, I will come back to you. There
is nothing in all the world so beautiful as your music.
When you cannot make it any more beautiful, then
come home, and you will find me waiting.*

Amaryllis

After that she was willing to study her French
hard in Paris. She was willing to learn all that the
English could show her about how to be dignified,
and how to be cordial, and how to be good-looking.
Then they came home. They left Peter to finish what

Cambridge had to teach him, because Peter was getting to be a man, and his father said he was very worth while and he must have at least two years of British training, because, after all, the British really are older than we are, and they have behind them a culture and a reverence for law and a nice way of doing things, and a precision of speech that would be very beneficial for Peter and all of us to begin to practice.

As for Amaryllis, she said she would take her lessons from a tutor. She was going home to wait for John Guido. It was only such a little while to wait now compared with all the years that had gone before. The papers had said how wonderfully he had played; that there was very little left for the great masters to teach him, and it was predicted that in a year or two more he would be ready to go before the world and play in any great auditorium in any great city. It was predicted that with the years he would be the equal of any violinist living and it might be, with the talent he evinced, that he could be the greatest.

"Of course he will!" said Amaryllis when she read the prediction. "Of course he will! After he comes home to the little house and the garden, after he learns where I am and how I have waited, something big and fine and splendid will grow up in his heart. Of course he will play better than anyone else ever has played! He will know how because he will have

the sunshine and the birds, he will have what the
flowers say to each other, little soft, whispery things
in his heart. We listened to them in the meadow.
He will have the flower talk to put in his music, and
he knows every last note that ever could be sung
down the whole length of Roaring Brook. Surely he
will play better than anyone else ever has played!"

So Amaryllis went home, and for several more
years she went straight ahead studying her own lessons, keeping her father's house, writing to Peter
half-motherly, half-sisterly letters, being the very
light of her father's eyes. During those two years, all
her spare time she lived in the little house. Those
were years when Amaryllis really grew. She was getting to be a woman now, very close to eighteen. She
had grown to woman's size. She had grown to woman's mental stature, and she had grown to beauty so
much greater than any beauty that could be seen in
girls around her that she shone out as one star
brighter than all the rest shines in the heavens, because she belonged to John Guido. She had kept
herself for him alone. Any healthful game she had
played. In races she had ridden. She could sail a boat
and she could swim, but there was not a boy living
who had dared lay his hands familiarly upon her. To
herself she was a sacred thing. She was set apart.
When she went to John Guido and said, "I have
come back to you," as she had promised, she must go
with lips that no other boy's kisses had touched. She

must go with ears that had not been sullied with vulgarity. She must go as God intended that every woman should go to the man she loves. She must go untouched by other men, unsullied, absolutely clean. And deep in her heart, Amaryllis knew that as she was planning to go to John Guido, he was coming to her. Those girls in Rome who had smiled on him and loitered in front of him, those girls who had beauty and youth and alluring charm—he had not even seen them. He had gone past them with his eyes looking clear across to America, looking only for Amaryllis. And when he came, there would not be any sordid story to tell him. There would not be anything humiliating to confess. She would be able to say,

"I have not gone with the crowd. I have waited apart. I have kept myself something sacred, something holy, waiting for you."

Amaryllis began putting her spirit into the little house in those days. A picture here, a book here, a rug, a bit of tapestry, a vase—she had forgotten just how it had looked in the beginning, how changed it would seem to its owners. She kept saying to herself,

"If the grass waves long, if the same flowers are blooming, a few more here and there where some have been crowded out, he won't feel he is coming to a strange, new place. He will be at home."

She had forgotten, when she put in a fountain here and a lilied pool there and stepping stones down flower-bordered trails, how changed it would seem. She only knew that she was creating beauty, and she knew that nowhere in all the world was there anyone who loved beauty more intensely than John Forrester and his boy. So Amaryllis waited, and she lived in beauty and she created beauty all through the alchemy of the love in her heart that was inspiring her, big and abundant, far reaching and deep seated, all the love that one loyal girl heart can possibly develop, first for the boy, and later for the man with whom some day she was going to be mated in love.

PART FOUR

The Yellow Cur

The Yellow Cur

THE world of the big island is never quite so lovely as it is in May when all the old pear trees and peach trees and apple trees are in bloom; when the wild flowers are brocading the meadows, and the buttercups are sheeting the swamps with gold and all around their margins grow the gold of celandine and the yellow lilies and the blue water hyacinths; when lush and rank the cattails and bulrushes are lifting; when the grass is brilliantly green and home-coming birds are shouting the ecstasy of their mating songs.

It was on a morning like this in the big house where Amaryllis reigned that she answered the telephone. She was standing in the front hall looking through the rooms, and she was smiling to think how homelike they were. When Paul Minton decided to lift both of his children from their environment and give them something entirely new, there had been selected for Amaryllis from her house the things she had loved, the things that were antiques and heirlooms in the family and that should be preserved, the things that she found comfortable and homelike and was happy with. Peter had brought the same kind of things from his house, and Paul Minton had brought from his apartment the furnishings that best fitted his curves and that he liked to look at and that had some value beyond money. When these things were fitted into the big house, it was not a house any more: it became a home. In some way the spirit on which that home was based had been made to extend to the people who were employed to care for it and to keep it alive. So Amaryllis was looking over her domain and feeling highly comfortable and pleased and happy.

She was wondering, as she wondered nearly every hour of every day of her life, what John Forrester and John Guido, his son, were going to think when they stepped into their home and found it changed. Amaryllis had to admit that they would find it changed. They would find it different, and she trembled as she stood there in the fear that she had gone too far, that she had done too much, that her tale of people who had leased the place and furnished it to suit themselves and then gone away and left the furnishings in part payment for the privilege of having used the place would not ring true. She wondered whether this tale were sufficiently plausible. The day before she had been at the little white house. With the addition of the studio and the adding of the music room, it did not seem small any more. With the green lifting in the lily pool and around the goldfish pond, with all the flowers sticking up their heads, with the perfume of apple blossoms sweetening the air, it seemed to Amaryllis that there was not a spot on all the great island that was so simple and so homelike, that gave such an invitation from the erect, prim little gate with its quaint latch, clear down to the last stepping stone beside the little brook that roared out of the Forrester land and on down across the meadows and the swamps until it reached the road and went on its way to the sea.

On a morning like this, with a world full of flowers and singing birds, and a heart full of love (and yet, by a unique paradox, hungry as ever for the love of a slip of a boy with big black eyes and crow-black blackness of hair and skillful hands and a heart overflowing with tenderness, a heart that had given love lavishly as it had received it) Amaryllis stood studying the situation. She did not exactly see how she could be surfeited with love and hungry for love at the same time. She could not think of a thing more to do for the little house of John Guido, but she thought perhaps if she went there and took a last look around, she might see something, because it was not going to be so very long now—not so very long.

She had been following John Guido from Rome to Berlin, from Berlin to Madrid, from Madrid to Paris, from Paris to London, and after London surely home would be next. It was at this point that the telephone rang. Because she was near it, Amaryllis answered it. The call was from the bank that handled Mr. Forrester's money and the leasing of his property. With one particular man who handled this particular business, Amaryllis had made friends. She had left instructions that he should keep her posted as to when the Forresters were coming, so that the supposed tenants might have time to move from the house.

When she answered the telephone, the voice of this particular man called for her and then went on to say that they had just received a letter informing them that on the twentieth of May the Forresters would be sailing. They wanted to go straight to their home, and they would be glad if the tenants could vacate it before that time.

In the ears of the particular man there echoed over the telephone wires the sweetest little laugh that he had ever heard, an ecstatic little thing, part a chuckle, part a gurgle, part a bird note, and part a young girl bubbling over with the ecstasy of living and loving. Then Amaryllis sobered down and tried to be quite businesslike. She said very primly that the tenants would have left the house and that the keys would have been turned in at the bank. They might cable Mr. Forrester to that effect. She cautioned the particular man, as she had cautioned him over and over again, not to grow definite; to remember, if any questions were asked concerning the tenants, precisely what it was that he was to say, and to remember that the Farleys, who had occupied the house, were very wealthy people who had greatly enjoyed the location, and anything they had done to it was merely part of their way of paying their lease. She thought that story was convincing. She did not see why it was not.

Then she hung up the receiver and stood still. Possibly in ten days more John Guido would be back to the garden of magic with the bed of striped grass, and the mystery of the meadow, and the song of the brook that grew so impetuous that men said it roared. Amaryllis came so near feeling as if she were going to fly that she lifted her feet and inspected them very carefully to see whether they might not have developed wings like those of Mercury in the mythology book.

Then she hurried to the nearest mirror and studied her face, first on one side and then on the other, and her brow and her eyes and her lips and her chin. She ran her fingers through her hair, hair that she had not cut as other girls were cutting their hair, because she could not possibly sacrifice those waves of sunshine until she knew whether John Guido wanted them as they were or some other way. He had loved her hair when she was that little bit of a thing who ran away from home and did not know any better than to lift her mouth and beg, as a hungry little bird in its nest begs for worms, of John Guido to give her the kisses that her mother had not cared to give and her father had neglected to give and her brother had not been taught to give. She looked at the mouth very carefully this morning. She must not do that any more. She must be very sedate and womanly now. John Guido had grown so tall that her head would not more than reach his shoulder. She would not ever again dare tell him that she was hungry. What she must do was to create a great hunger in his heart. He was a big man now. He must come to her and tell her that he was hungry.

That first time she had given a definite promise that she would go back to him; after that she must not go again. But back she was going as soon as she knew that he was there, as soon as she was sure that he would meet her in the garden, back for one golden day, probably early in June, she was going back to him. And after that she was not going any more until she went to stay, because, in her heart, to Amaryllis the little white house and the garden of love were home.

She did not know just what her father and Peter were going to do without her. She had made herself very essential to her father and Peter, because her heart, so utterly starved in the beginning, had sucked up love as the parched desert sucks up rain. She had flourished under love as the desert flourishes under rain. But so had Paul Minton, and so had Peter.

That night, when Paul Minton came home, Amaryllis was waiting for him halfway down the drive. She made a flying leap that landed her on the running board of his car and opened her lips. Before she had time to say a word, her father had closed them with a kiss, and what he said was, "Cable today. Peter will be here in about ten days."

Then, in excitement so tense that neither of them were very particularly articulate, they discovered that the same boat was going to bring Peter home and John Guido and Mr. Forrester. There was a meager possibility that at some time in the length of a voyage on that boat they might run across one another and might become acquainted.

Amaryllis thought about it all night when she should have been sleeping. The next day Peter had a cable that read:

Delighted. Same boat an artist, John Forrester; his son, a violinist. Want you to be good friends. Get acquainted with younger Forrester, but do not mention me. Secret. Tell you later.

That was the biggest cable that Amaryllis had ever paid for, and it made an awful hole in her allowance because, when she got through buying books and rugs and the singing birds in gold cages that

Marie was taking care of in the house of John Forrester, there was so little allowance left that she wore
the same dress oftener than any other girl who came
from a big house such as Amaryllis lived in. She did
not buy nearly such expensive dresses as she might
have bought if she had not been buying such a number of other things because she had to keep doing
something for John Guido or be sick abed with
longing for him.

Then followed ten days that were the busiest of
all Amaryllis's life. Paul Minton sympathized with
her and helped her. Peter's room was made especially
fine, and some new pieces of furniture were put in it.
Peter's horse was groomed until a reflection could
be seen in its shining flanks, and Peter's dogs were
taken care of a little more particularly than they had
been ten days before.

Paul Minton went with Amaryllis over to the little
white house, and he was shocked at the expenditure
he had permitted and entranced with the result.
There was no question but that Amaryllis had the
homemaking instinct. She had the touch, the divine
home touch. Just at that minute it seemed to Paul
Minton that there was something sacred about
money when it could materialize a picture so exquisite as the little white house now made with the
graceful wing for the artist and one of equal grace
for the musician, with the old apple trees leaning at
different angles and lifting up their branches loaded

with sweetness, the grass beneath them brocaded with blue violets and moss magic. He had to admit that he had not seen anything anywhere that seemed so quiet, so serenely still, and so entrancingly sweet. Perhaps the highest tribute he paid her work was when he put his arms around Amaryllis and said "Amarylly,"—because that was his own private and personal pet name for her—"Amarylly, I am all sort of breathless here. I feel as if I should walk on tiptoe and whisper."

Amaryllis threw her arms around his neck and hugged him tight and her eyes were wet.

Close to his ear she said it low, "You'd just better do it, Dad! You'd just better whisper, because Love is asleep here, and when it wakes up, oh, boy! there are going to be music and song and laughter and there are going to be little people and the brightest sunshine that this old island ever knew when Love wakes up in this little white house!"

Then they went home, and Amaryllis went into the library and into her father's quarters to see what she could do for him. Just as she came out, she caught him squarely coming from her own particular suite of rooms. When she looked at him inquiringly, he said,

"Amarylly, I was just casting my optics around to see if I could figure on anything else that I could put into your rooms that you would like to have. Could you help your old Dad?"

Amaryllis laughed and said, "Dad, don't let your affection take the form of spending more money on me. All I want you to do is just to love me. There isn't anything in the world that I need in my rooms that I haven't got."

Then Amaryllis went up to her father and slipped her hands up his breast to the base of his neck on each side and bore down hard, a little way she had of getting his particular attention. Very softly, almost whispery, she said,

"Father, do you suppose that she, do you suppose that Mother has anything in her life so precious as the thing we have? Do you suppose she's got love like ours?"

She could feel her father's frame grow tense under her fingers. She could feel him grow taller. She could sense a roughness in his voice. He stood very still a minute and then he said,

"No, Amarylly, I don't think she has. Truly, I don't think she would want it. I think when she was made something was left out of her, or it was neglected when she was very tiny. I know that she would not care for what we do. She only cares for fine clothes and jewels and to be worshiped."

"Sometimes," said Amaryllis, "I feel as if maybe we had not served her right, as if maybe we should have gone to her and tried to force her to see our way."

Paul Minton laid his hands on Amaryllis's shoulders and held her very tight.

"Amaryllis," he said, "do you remember one time when I went away on business and was gone nearly a month and did not leave you any address because I said I would be traveling constantly? Well, Amaryllis, I went to France and I hunted up your mother and I tried to tell her and I tried with all my heart and brain to get her to come back. But she did not want us, Amaryllis. She did not want anything we had to offer. She did not want me. She did not want you and Peter. She did not want this country. We won't ever mention it again, but you can feel your heart clean on that score. She has had her great chance and scorned it. May God bless and save her and her count."

Then he bent his head and kissed Amaryllis very hard on the lips and turned and went to his own room. As she stood and watched him, she noticed that his shoulders sagged a little and that his head was bent slightly, and that it was growing very white. She realized that, love him as she might, think of him as she would, she was not going to be able to give him what she had to give John Guido. While he was young and while he was strong, there was no woman to bring to him her richest gifts of the heart and of the mind. Was he all the rest of his life to be a man defrauded, a man bereft of what it was his right to have? Amaryllis ran after him and opened the door. She found him before his desk with his arms crossed and his head laid on them. She lifted up his arms and hopped on the desk and made a pillow of her lap to rest his head in. She combed her fingers through his hair, and very unsteadily she said,

"Dad, why don't you look around among the women you know? Why don't you see if somewhere you don't know one, or you can't find one, who would give to you what I am going to give to John Guido when he comes? Why don't you, Dad?"

Paul Minton sat back in his chair and lifted his head and looked at Amaryllis with eyes of astonishment.

"Amaryllis," he said, "the temptation has been big and strong for a good many years, but I so defrauded you in the beginning of your life, I was not going to take any risks of making anything unpleasant for you the rest of the way. So I would not risk it. I would not risk the chance of any woman living making you unhappy again, Amarylly. Not in the same house with you. If you are willing, after you go to John Guido, and maybe after Peter decides to select some charming girl and move back to his house, then maybe I might make the venture."

Amaryllis slid from the table and stood between his knees and kissed him over and over and said,

"Don't wait, Dad. If you know anyone, if there is

one single woman you are dead sure about, one who loves the things we love, go and get her, bring her today, for all I care!"

But Paul Minton shook his head.

"You youngsters are too impetuous for me," he said. "I'll go slowly. I'll think about it, and if I am too lonely after you leave me, why then I'll see what I can do."

Amaryllis said, "That's a promise, Dad?"

And he answered her, "Yes, that's a promise."

Then one of the impulses that made Amaryllis so altogether adorable moved her heart, and she slipped her hand into his and said,

"I wish I could go with you, Dad. Oh, I wish I could see her with my own eyes! I wish I could see her home and how she lives. I wish I could see if I could make her love me a little bit. I wish I could be satisfied and sure in my own heart that she does love you, before you do anything that you could not take back."

Paul Minton put his arms around Amaryllis so tight that he tried her small frame, and he kissed her so hard that she felt that kiss half an hour afterward. He said,

"I wonder to my soul if that young rascal has got the proper idea of exactly the kind of a girl that he is going to have the chance to win!"

And Amaryllis laughed because that was such a joke. The idea that John Guido might not appreciate her! All she had to do was to shut her eyes and remember him as he had stood before a packed house in Rome, remember the smile on his lips and the toss of his head, the way he had looked and what he had put into the notes of his violin when he played "Amaryllis."

So she laughed up at her father and she said, "Do you remember how he played 'Amaryllis'? If he could play me like that, don't you worry, Dad! Don't you worry! There won't be any trouble about John Guido not appreciating me."

The remainder of those ten days Amaryllis never remembered exactly how she lived through. She went to the dock alone to meet Peter's boat. She promised her father to bring him straight to the office. She went alone because she had a secret in her heart, a secret about that cable. She had not told her father that there was a possibility that Peter might have made friends with John Guido and they might leave the boat together. She did not want to meet John Guido on a dock, in a crowd of people, before Peter. She could not endure that. She could not meet him anywhere for the first time except in the wayward garden of magic. She could not meet him anywhere that she could not shout to him, "John Guido, I've come back! I've come back to you!" She could not meet him anywhere that she could not rush into his arms and lay her head over his heart and cry if she wanted to, cry until her face was all tear smeary and her nose all shiny and her eyes all red. She would not care what she did when she met John Guido. She meant to do whatever she felt like doing.

So she wore a very long coat with a very high collar and a very much pulled down hat and a very heavy veil. Peter would not have known her if he had been told that she was Amaryllis. Off at one side, as close as she dared come, she stood, watching and waiting, and presently, right over and upside down, with a skip and a jump and a pirouette and a whirl and a leap, oh, the things her heart did, things it never had done before in all her life! She had guessed right! Peter had found John Guido. They had made friends. Down the gangplank together they came, and my! but they were fine young men! Peter had grown so! He seemed so tall for Peter, and his clothing had such a distinguished look. She was so proud of Peter! She swept him with one comprehensive glance, then leaned back against whoever it was that was behind her with little gasps of ecstasy slipping between her lips, because, after all, your brother is your brother, but beside the brother there was John Guido!

And *he* had grown, oh! so tall! He had grown so handsome! His eyes were shining with such a happy light, and he was laughing as he talked. He was turning his head to say things to John Forrester, looking big and fine behind him as they came down the gangway. They were not very many yards from her when they stopped and Peter shook hands with both of them.

He said, "Our car is always parked across here. Our driver knows where to come for me, and it is just possible that my dad or my sister will be in the car waiting. So I'll go. But remember, John, you are to come on Monday for that party on my yacht that I am going to give to the fellows as my welcome home. We will take a run up the coast, maybe up in the direction of Maine. Maybe there will be some hunting or some fishing. I don't know what we will want to do, but the world's in spring, the weather is fine, and isn't it wonderful to be back home again?"

John Guido laid his hand on Peter's shoulder and said, "Thank you. I will be wherever you tell me to meet you. I shall love to go on your yachting party with you. I will bring my violin along if you say so, and I'll make it talk to the fellows while we are having our party, and I know it will be great!"

Then they shook hands all over again, and Peter turned in the direction that he expected to find the car waiting. John Guido and his father turned toward the taxicabs, and distinctly Amaryllis heard John Forrester say, "First thing we do we'll go to the bank and get the keys to the little old place."

John Guido answered, "I hope we find it exactly the way we left it."

Then they were gone. Amaryllis was rather dazed,

but she could not feel that John Guido would not like what she had done. She could not feel that he would not be enchanted when he saw the little house and the garden, after he had had a day or two to become accustomed to the change, maybe. Then she turned and went rushing after Peter. She overtook him and fell into his arms and the first words he said were, "Well, my word! Why the disguise?"

Amaryllis laughed and said, "Because I did not want anyone to know me."

"And why the mysterious cablegram?" asked Peter.

"Wasn't he nice?" cried Amaryllis breathlessly as she plastered a few more kisses on Peter and stepped back really to get the look of him and the feel of him.

"I'll tell the world he is topnotch!" said Peter. "He is just the rarest chap that I ever met. But, Amaryllis, if you've got any idea that you can get your tentacles on that man, you had better forget it."

Amaryllis said, "What makes you think that, Peter?"

"Why, Amaryllis," said Peter, "that chap is so dead in love with some girl he's waiting for that he can't see any other girl. There wasn't a marriageable female on that ship who did not throw herself at his head from the time he stepped on the promenade deck until he came down the gangplank, and he didn't even see them! Amaryllis, he's so dead in love with some girl somewhere that he'll not even talk about her. All he *will* do is to talk about *love*. It is a thing so high, so holy, and so wonderful! He is going to get his trunks unpacked and get settled in his house. He is going to take this little run with me the first of the week, and then he is going back to his house to sit down and wait for love that has promised to come to him. I could hardly get him to agree to go with me for three days, but he did finally consent for that long because I begged so hard. I don't know why you wanted me to make friends with him, but you've surely got good judgment. Where did you meet him?"

Amaryllis laughed.

"I'll tell you all about it some day," she promised. "Never mind about it now."

She could not very well tell him anything that minute. She was trying frantically to figure what day it was, and how long three days more would be; on what day it would be reasonable and decent to keep her promise to go back to the little white house and the Magic Garden. Now was Saturday. Sunday to reach home and unpack. Monday, Tuesday, and Wednesday for the three days' yacht trip. Thursday? Could she go to the garden that coming Thursday? There was nothing particularly wearisome about riding in Peter's yacht. It was a boat de luxe. All his friends were crazy over it. He handled it extremely well, because Peter was slow, he was deliberate, he was bulldog stubborn, and when he undertook to do a thing, he did it thoroughly. When she could go would have to depend on when the yacht came in. Whenever Peter came home, John Guido would be at home.

She asked Peter a question.

"Peter," she said, "one time in the cabin on your boat I saw a picture of me. Is it there yet?"

"Sure it is!" said Peter promptly. "And it's going to stay right there, and if ever I find a girl I want to marry, she can have a place beside it. She can't have the place you've always had since I've owned that boat! Nobody but you can ever have it!"

"Peter," said Amaryllis, "do you truly love me?"

"Yes," said Peter, "I do. I love you more than any man I know loves his sister. Anything you want, anything I can do for you, Amaryllis, I'll try to do. I don't know that I've ever talked about it but that time you got around Dad and made him give us a real home and lifted me out of the kind of hell that I was stewing in, eaten up with homesickness and hunger and longing, and brooding on things I did not understand, with no right exercise and only one boy friend on earth—God knows, Amaryllis, you saved me from being something horrible! I might have gone crazy. I might have lost my reason and become a horrid thing if it hadn't been for you. Any time there is anything I can do, anything for you, little sister, let me know."

Very promptly Amaryllis said, "All right, Peter. On Monday, when you board your yacht, go straight to your room and take that picture of me and put it in the bottom of a drawer, down deep under your shirts somewhere so that none of your friends will see it if they should happen to come to your cabin."

"Yes, I will—*not!*" said Peter.

"Then I like your sincerity!" said Amaryllis. "You tell me you will do anything for me, and then refuse to lay away my photograph for only three days! Couldn't I have a special reason?"

"Oh-ho!" said Peter. "So *that's* the way the wind blows! Your reason has got something to do with your mysterious cable, has it? Oh, well, then, for three days, at your own behest, I'll put you away, but I think it's kind of a rotten thing you ask me to do, because the fellows do come to my cabin. All I am asking have been on the yacht before, except John Guido Forrester. They come in once in a while, just one or two at a time, to lounge and have a chance to talk personally a little, and I am rather proud of my pretty sister."

"But you are going to do it, Peter? You aren't going to forget?" urged Amaryllis.

"I am going to do it," promised Peter. "I won't forget, because I'll remember that there's a reason that I am to be told one of these days."

"And if you can steer those boys off the subject of me, if you can head them off when they go to talking about girls, if there is any way you can keep them from mentioning me, I'd be awfully glad. I don't want anything said about a girl named Amaryllis before John Guido."

"I'll do my best," said Peter. "I'll do my best. But you're handing me something of a contract. I am going to be a man with something on my mind; and I've grubbed so hard that I wanted for these three days to have a mind at ease, because you know, Amaryllis, after I've had a short vacation, I'm going in the office one morning and pull off my coat and roll up my sleeves, and I am going to surprise our dad. I'm going to square up to him and say, 'Now, Dad, I'm a man. What's my job?' And I'm going to work."

"But, Peter!" cried Amaryllis, "with all Grandfather's money?"

"Oh, yes, I know," said Peter, "but his money isn't *my* money. I notice you call it his. *I* didn't earn it. It doesn't represent anything *I* did. I can see that you have boy on the brain. You must prepare yourself for the fact that I might get *girl* on the brain, and if I do, I want to have something to offer her that I did myself, something that means *me*. I am not very keen on saying, 'Darling, I love you. Will you marry me and move into the house my grandfather built and help me spend the money my grandfather gave me?' I would like to be able to have a little coin of the realm that I had amassed myself. I think I can find something to do with Grandfather's money. I don't know what yet. Maybe I'll need some of it, but I am going to have something that I earn myself."

"Good for you, Peter!" said Amaryllis. "I like that school you've been going to. I like the way you speak. I like the way you carry yourself. I like your clothes. I think Dad hit it off just right when he sent you there for two years. You've got something that is fine, that most of our boys this side haven't learned. Now, when you add to it the best of what we have over here, why, don't you see, you are going to be a good deal of a man, Peter?"

"I intend to try to be," said Peter.

By that time they were at Mr. Minton's office, and together they went to him. He closed business for the day and went home with them because he was so pleased over Peter he could not let him out of his sight. He had to look at him, and feel his muscle, and listen to him talk. Peter could not help seeing how genuinely pleased his father was. He forgot about the vacation he was planning to have, and they had not more than reached home and gotten a little bit of the first exuberance of meeting over until Peter, never waiting for the vacation or the walk in the office, or the coat shedding, said, "Dad, anywhere in your business, is there a place for me?"

Paul Minton said, "Why, Peter, with what I have amassed and what your grandfather left you——"

And Peter said, "Oh, hang what you have

amassed! Where does that get me? And what Grandfather left me can stay left for a while until we see
how and where we had better use it. What I want is
something that *I* have earned, something that repre-
sents *me*."

Mr. Paul Minton said, "Well, Peter, you have
made this a fine day for me! I'll tell you that! I've
often wondered if you were going to become one of
these tea-drinking lounge lizards that I came fairly
close to being myself for a time. I have often wondered. You can be very sure there is a place for you,
and there is work for you. You may be very, very
sure."

So they were all inexpressibly happy, and Peter
and Amaryllis took the car and went flying over the
island to find Peter's one best friend and to say
"How-do-you-do?" to later friends, to greet friends
of Amaryllis, and it was not any time at all until
Monday morning came and the car rolled away from
the door with Peter in it going to gather up half a
dozen men for a first trial run for the season on the
beautiful yacht that was the pride of Peter's heart.

From the steps Amaryllis threw kisses and waved
him a last good-by. She wondered how she was going
to endure three long days. Suddenly she decided. She
had been skimping, and saving, and spending every
cent of her allowance and every penny she could get
in any other way on John Guido. Her clothes really
were almost shabby. She would go into the big city

and she would buy the very prettiest things that she could find. She would make herself lovely for John Guido. She should have been about it long ago. Dressmakers should have been busy, but she reflected that miracles could be performed in the little shops of New York. If she went to a shop that she always patronized and told Madame a tale about a sudden need that had arisen, she could devise the kind of a dress that would be the most suitable dress in which to come up the path of stepping stones beside the roaring brook and into the Magic Garden.

Amaryllis had made up her mind what she was going to do. As soon as Peter came home—if he came in the evening, then early the following morning—she was going to call John Guido on the telephone and she was going to ask him if at ten o'clock he would be beside the syringa at the bed of striped grass in the Magic Garden. She had put a beautiful bench of stone with a back and arm rests skillfully carved, with the striped grass coming up all around it and the syringa, which would be white with bloom now, hanging over it. Perhaps the apple trees would still be pink. The pear trees would be in their prime. The cherries and plums would be over, but the wild plums down in the meadow would still be blooming, and the wild crab, a mystery of pink-flushed sweetness.

Amaryllis drew a deep breath. All she was going to ask him was if at ten o'clock he would be at the bed of striped grass. Then she was going to hang up quickly. She was going to walk alone beside Roaring Brook and across the meadow and come up to the foot of the garden; and at the stone bench John Guido would be waiting for her. She would have kept her promise. All she meant to say was, "John Guido, I've come back to you!" After that, everything would be up to him.

That was a beautiful plan, and she had the greatest success with the dresses. Her eyes were so very bright and her cheeks were so pink and she looked so adorable in anything Madame tried on her that she inspired the modiste to the height of her creative art. There was no difficulty at all in being extravagant, because Madame knew that ordinarily Amaryllis was not extravagant. This time she understood from the shining eyes and the flushed cheeks that here was an especial occasion, and it behooved her to do her level best. So she held her head between her hands and thought and thought; and Amaryllis explained about the garden and the syringa bush and the bench.

"A garden party?" asked Madame.

"Yes, but in the morning," answered Amaryllis. "It begins in the morning. It begins about ten o'clock in the morning."

So together they studied out the loveliest dress that ever could be thought of, a dress of lightest weave, of the palest blue in the most delicate mate-

rial that Madame could produce. There were to be
sleeves of chiffon and embroidery and little touches
of color. There was to be a big hat with a droopy
plume. There were to be flowers and laces. There
were to be shoes and stockings to match.

Then there were other dresses. There was one
that *had* to go along. It had to stay in the car and
come around to the front entrance with the driver
after Amaryllis had started up the Roaring Brook on
foot. This dress had to be of silver chiffons and
faintly silver lace. There must be iridescent beads
like the inner lining of a pearl shell, because this
dress had to be slipped on to dance before the
Amaryllis urn in the moonlight to the music that
John Guido would make, and maybe, if John Forrester was very nice, they would let him come and
watch it from the bench beside the striped grass.

Then Amaryllis went home to wait. She did not
know how she was going to live through Tuesday
and Wednesday. On Tuesday morning she had decided that, after her bath and breakfast, she would
go in her car to visit some of her friends, do something to try to shorten the day. So she put on a sport
suit of fine white cloth. There was a bit of gold in
the braid and a touch of blue and a touch of pink
here and there. As she stood before the mirror and
set the hat that she meant to wear on her curly head
and looked at her image, she reflected that John
Guido might perhaps like her in that dress. So she

went down to breakfast and, as she left the table, she gave the order for her car to be brought around.

In the hall she met the footman. He looked so white that Amaryllis stopped before him. She noticed that he had put something behind his back. She stretched out her hand.

"The morning paper, Johnson?" she asked.

Johnson bowed.

"There is something in it you do not want me to see?"

Johnson caught his breath and said, "I don't know what to do, Miss! I don't know what I should do!"

"Give me the paper," said Amaryllis, "and show me what it is."

Johnson handed her the paper and in big lines across the top of it there smote her in the face:

YACHT OF A YOUNG MILLIONAIRE
WRECKED OFF COAST OF MAINE.
NO PARTICULARS. ALL ON
BOARD LOST

Amaryllis looked at the paper and she looked at Johnson.

Then she said quietly, "Telephone Father to see this paper and tell him that I am going to Mr. Forrester. If you can't remember the name, write it down."

She walked out of the front door and down the steps and gave the directions to the little house. All the way she sat staring at the paper that she held in her hands, because that was her work. If she had not asked Peter to make friends with John Guido, if she had not asked him to hunt him up, if she had not urged him to take him along—at that minute he would have been safe at home with his father at the little house there in the garden.

There were no tears in Amaryllis' eyes. They just got bigger and bigger and brighter and brighter, and all the lovely color washed out of her cheeks and out of her lips, and all she could do was to grip that awful paper and stare at those awful words. June never had a more glorious morning, but Amaryllis saw none of its glory. Once she called to the driver, "Can't you make a little time? I am in a very great hurry!"

After that the car jolted a bit, and by and by it stopped at the gate—the gate that she had copied so faithfully from the old gate that used to hang by one hinge. She had herself selected the new hinges and the latch. She opened it now and went through and down the walk between the flowers, on either side a bright array of soft, delicate colour, and here and there the flame of a red lily opened to the sun, an early amaryllis.

As she came up the steps and crossed the veranda she found that suddenly she was trembling. Her knees were wavering under her, but she reached the bell. Then she leaned against the screen until John

Forrester himself came from his studio and crossed the living room. She had to step back that the screen might be opened, but she swayed so that she almost fell. He took one long look at her and at the paper she was clutching, and then he put his arm around her and helped her inside. He helped her to a big chair. Then he drew up another one and sat down before her and looked at her very carefully.

He said, "If I am not mistaken, you are the little girl grown tall who promised my boy, John Guido, that she would come back to him."

Amaryllis said nothing because she could not speak. It was all she could do to make a stiff neck nod her head enough that John Forrester would understand that she meant an affirmative.

John Forrester reached up and lifted the hat from her head and took the paper from her hands and said, "My dear, have you any conception of how my boy has idolized you and idealized you? Will it please you to know that he has not followed the ways of a good many young men? Will you be glad to have his father tell you that no woman has touched his life or his heart but you?"

"Don't," said Amaryllis. "Oh, my God! Don't! I can't bear it!"

And because it was the only thing she could think of to do, she shoved the paper at him. He picked it up and read it.

Then slowly his face began to whiten and he said

to her, "Does this mean that the yacht that has gone down is the one that John Guido sailed on? The Minton yacht? The one belonging to that nice youngster my boy made friends with coming over?"

Amaryllis nodded her head.

Then she gasped, "Yes, Peter. My brother Peter."

John Forrester held her hands tighter and bowed his head and for a long time they sat very still holding tight to each other. Finally Amaryllis straightened up in the chair.

She said, "You had better let go my hands now. In a minute you won't want to hold them. You won't want ever to see me again as long as I live."

There was not much intelligence in the eyes John Forrester trained on her. He did not get much of the import of what she was saying. Something about releasing her hands. So she tried to draw them away, and when he saw that she wanted them released, he let them go. Then she clutched them together so tight that the joints grew white and she looked so little and she looked so stricken all he could think of to say was, "Tell me."

So, in panting gusts, she managed it. Just the bare, crude facts.

"I sent him," she said. "I wanted Peter to know him. I wanted Peter and Father to love him. I thought if Peter made friends with him on the boat and they came across together, he could come to the house to see Peter, and then Father would know him and they would like him and we could all be friends."

Slowly John Forrester nodded.

"I see," he said.

"I wanted," gasped Amaryllis, "I wanted everybody to love him the way I did, and on Thursday—on Thursday morning—I was going to call him on the telephone and tell him that at ten o'clock I would come across the meadow and into the garden where we had such good times. I would come back to him as I promised that day the policeman took me away from him. I was going to come back only once. I was trying to fix a way before I came so that after that he could come to *me*. You see, don't you?"

"Yes, I see," said John Forrester. "I see."

"And now you will always hate me. Now——" She paused a long time and then she looked at him. "I don't know," she said, "if it makes much difference if you do hate me. I don't know that anything makes any difference. Everything is ruined. It wasn't any use, not any of this, nor any of anything. It isn't any use that every hour of every day I have loved him. It isn't any use that I tried so hard to be a good girl and a nice girl, the kind of a girl that his mother was. I wanted you to love me. I wanted you to love me as well as John Guido. And now you will only hate me."

"For God's sake, don't!" cried John Forrester, and he came crashing down on his knees in front of her and put his arms around her. Then both of them began to cry—Amaryllis, little shrill, sharp panting cries; John Forrester, deep, wrenching sobs that tore up through his body and shook him and twisted him. They clung together until they were exhausted. After a long time, Amaryllis tried to find a handkerchief and wipe her face.

"Will you ever," she asked, "will you ever forgive me? Will you ever in all this world see me again without hating me?"

"Don't," said John Forrester. "It wasn't your fault. There was nothing in your heart for my boy but love. I could not hate you. No one could hate you. You must not even think such a thing. You must not say it. There couldn't be any question of hating you. There hasn't been any hour of any day since they took you away that John Guido has not been teaching me, by word, by example, how to love you. Don't let yourself think it could be any other way."

"But I've got to think," said Amaryllis. "I've got to think because, you see, nothing can alter the fact that I did it. If I had not sent the cable to Peter asking him to make friends with John Guido on the boat they might never have known each other. You see, you can't get away from the fact that I did it. I never meant to tell you. I never meant you to know. I was the tenant you had here. There isn't a new flower growing that I did not set, most of them with my own hands. I planned the music room and I planned the studio, because I had to do something to keep from dying until he got back. I had to keep doing something for him every day. You see, don't you?"

"Yes, I see," said John Forrester. "I see. It was like that with him. He studied for you. He played for you! He quit work only long enough to take sufficient exercise to keep him fit for you. I see."

He could not say anything more because there did not seem to be anything more to say. But once Amaryllis started talking, she did not seem to be able to stop.

"I didn't plan the party," she said. "Peter planned that because Peter loved his boat so. He thought it was the most wonderful boat, and he loved to sail it himself, and he did it so well. I can't imagine what happened. I haven't been able to read what happened."

"Wait," said John Forrester. "Give me that paper. Let me see what it really does say."

So he took the paper in shaking hands and sat down and read through the account of the disaster. When he had finished he shook his head.

"It happened in the night," he said. "An explosion in the engine room. The boat was literally torn to pieces. A few fragments washed ashore. The name and the number were on one of them. Something in the engine room. An explosion of some kind. I don't believe it is possible that anyone will ever know."

Amaryllis stood up.

"They won't get them?" she said. "They won't bring them home? We can't even have what's left of Peter and John Guido?"

"If this paper is right, no," said John Forrester. "We can't even lay them where we can go to them. We will have to think of them as sleeping away down deep in the cold, clean water of the sea."

"Oh, I can't!" cried Amaryllis. "I can't! I can't have Peter gone like that! I can't lose John Guido without a touch, without a word. Oh, the wonderful, wonderful man! I can't have horrors happen to him. And those other boys, all those other boys, they've got mothers, fathers, and sisters, and they've got sweethearts. There was Billy Barthol. What's Jane Price going to say when she knows Billy Barthol is never coming again? It was like that with nearly every one of them. I don't know one of those boys whom some girl did not love. I don't believe any one of them was all by himself so that there isn't someone to be hurt. I can't stand it! All their friends will all wish they hadn't gone. They will all blame Peter for taking them. I don't think I can endure it, not any way at all!"

John Forrester took Amaryllis in his arms and held her tight.

"Hush!" he said. "Hush! Try not to think. See if you can't just live for a little while. Your perspective is all twisted. No one could blame Peter. They were all *glad* to go. There was just one thing in the world that worried John Guido about going. He was crazy to go. He had never been on a private yacht like that. He had never had a treat like that in all his life with other young men. All that worried him was that he was afraid to leave the garden for fear you would know he was here, and that you might come when he was gone. He did not know what you knew about him, but the night of the concert in Rome he almost went crazy when he had the red lilies from you and the note, and knew that you had seen him and gone away on account of his work and left him without a word. That almost killed him, and it almost killed me. After that he played, my God! how he played. That violin sobbed and it laughed and it danced and it sang! Such playing I have never heard in all this world as John Guido played after he knew that you had been to Rome, knew that you had heard him play 'Amaryllis.' "

Amaryllis lifted her head.

"Straight across the street. Did you, about that time, ever notice a big car standing by the day?"

"Yes, we did," said John Forrester. "We noticed it and we talked about it."

"As long as it stood there," said Amaryllis, "I was in the second story of the little house across the street. I was behind the curtain watching when John Guido went down to the street for the paper or brought in the milk, or the fruit, or the flowers. One day, in the market place, I followed him and I saw him buy a big bunch of amaryllis. I saw him bury his face in the lilies. I saw how the lovely girls of Rome and the tourist girls and the travelers looked at him as he passed on the streets. I saw how they smiled at him, but he saw only his lilies. Oh, I could not have endured it much longer if I had not seen him with the lilies. That night, while he played 'Amaryllis,' Father held me tight in his arms. I could not have stood not to go to him that night if Father had not held me tight. And now I am not ever going to see him at all! I don't think I can live! Mr. John Forrester, do you think I can go on living?"

John Forrester held her tight and said, "Yes, Amaryllis, you can. But you must take it a day at a time. I don't think John Guido loved you more than I loved his mother, and I had to see her leave me, a little thing, a thing of beauty, see her go out alone in the night in the dark. She was afraid and she clung to me, but I had to see her go, and I have had to live on all these years without her. Yes, Amaryllis, you can endure it. There will be work you can do. There will be someone you can comfort. There will be some way. I have had my pictures and my boy. We will have to find something that will make life bearable for you."

Amaryllis drew away her hands and stood up. She stood very straight, and she looked so little and so stricken that John Forrester's heart ached for her as badly as it ached for himself.

"Well," she said, "wherever he is, he knows that I have kept my promise. He knows that I did all I knew how to make his house smile for him when he came home."

She stopped and turned straight toward John Forrester.

"Did he know?" she asked. "Did he guess?"

A twisted smile ran across John Forrester's face.

"Why, surely we knew," he said. "Of course we guessed. Nothing in all the world could do the thing that you have done here, Amaryllis, but personal love. There isn't any such thing as a tenant who would come into a house and put rest and peace and serenity of spirit and beauty, such beauty of color and form! and such convenience and comfort, as you have put here. No tenant could put love like that into a house, and those red lilies everywhere until they flamed love to heaven! You couldn't look to the right or to the left; you couldn't look out or across without the whole landscape crying 'Amaryllis!' at you. We hadn't reached the front door before we knew that Amaryllis had set her mark all over the place."

Amaryllis tried to smile.

"I'm so glad," she said. "Oh, I am so glad that he knew! I am so glad."

"He had the spot selected where he thought you

would come. He thought you would come down in the garden beside a bed of striped grass where he made the flower doll ladies for you. He found the bench there with the little cupids on it and garlands of roses, and he found the platform that you had made to dance the 'Amaryllis' dance on, and the urn with the lilies. He found them, and he knew. Nothing ever could have induced him to go except the thought that you would not know when he was here; that it would take you some time to find out that he had come home. You were to come to him. He thought there would be plenty of time for him to slip away for three days before you would know we had arrived. He didn't know his new friend was your brother, but I did. That was why I urged him to go."

John Forrester stopped, and Amaryllis stopped, and they looked at each other.

"I haven't said it yet," said Amaryllis at last, "but I've got to begin saying it now. I can't keep it back any longer. Why? Why? I have tried to be a good girl. Every single night I have said the prayer he taught me. Some way, Father got the last two lines from John Guido for me. Every single night on my knees I've prayed that prayer. I haven't been selfish. I haven't been wicked. I have given away all I had to give. I haven't worn expensive clothing as the other girls have. I have tried to be good, and I don't call this much of a reward. I wasn't working for re-

ward, either, unless you could call John Guido a reward. Of course, he would have been that. Of course,
he would. But I can't think *why*. I can't think *why!*"

John Forrester took her in his arms again and
turned her face against his breast and covered her
head, as much as he could shield it, with his hand,
and held her tight.

He said, "Amaryllis, if there is one word above
all other words that have been shouted up to the
face of heaven day and night ever since man and
woman learned love and learned language and
learned grief, it is just that one little word 'Why?'
I suspect the Almighty is more wearied with hearing
'Why?' than any other word that men and women
ever fling at Him from this beautiful world where
dark days will come and trouble will creep in and
death will cut down. You know that old saying,
'Death loves a shining mark?' That is what John
Guido was. That is what your brother Peter was, and
all those other boys. I sat near enough to hear them
talk on board often. They were sane; they were
clean. They were fine men. Your brother meant to
go into business with his father. He meant to make
a way for himself. He meant to do something that
would help the country and the poor and the strug-
gling with the millions that his grandfather left him.
They talked it over. He meant to have something
that he had earned himself to offer the girl he loved.

John Guido had his music. There was a fortune in his violin, in his fingers, and he had his brain and his wonderful love to offer you."

"And his violin has gone, too," wailed Amaryllis. "I heard him say he was going to take the violin along, so that's gone, too!"

"Never mind about the violin," said John Forrester. "Wherever John Guido is, that is where it should be. I would not ever want anyone else to play it after I've heard him play it, after the voices he put into it. I couldn't bear having anyone else play it. I'm glad that it went with him."

Amaryllis lifted up her face and said, "Mr. John Forrester, will you tell me once again that you don't hate me? Will you kiss me good-by? Will you take me out and put me in my car? I must go to Father now. You see, I came to you first. I had to come to you first. But now I must go to my father, because my father loved his son just as you loved yours."

"Yes," said John Forrester. "And you will come again, Amaryllis? You will come whenever you can, and you will let me come to you?"

"If you only will," said Amaryllis. "If you only will!"

"And about that forgiveness," said John Forrester. "Forget it, Amaryllis. Don't ever mention it again. The boy was proud to go, happy to go, and I was proud to have him. I thought it meant that he was making friends of the right kind. To tell you the truth, when they talked about it on the boat, he would not promise to go, he would not consent to go. I knew what was in his heart. I knew that he was afraid to go. Really he went because I urged him to, on account of what I knew and surmised about Peter. I wanted him to make friends among business-men and outdoor men. I wanted him to make friends who were not interested in music as he was. I did not want him to be so one-sided. I did not want him to be obsessed with one idea, to spend his life on one thing. It was my fault, really, that he went. All he wanted to do was to come to the house and the gar-den that you had promised to come back to and wait for you."

"And now he will not ever come! He will not ever come! What shall I do?" wailed Amaryllis. "What shall I do?"

Just then, at the same time, both of them heard it, away in the distance, a little bit of a note, a faint little bit of a note. They could not believe it at all. Amaryllis stiffened in John Forrester's arms, and John Forrester gripped her enough to almost break her bones. Both of them turned their faces toward the garden. Both of them heard the click of the latch, and then, soft and easy, a note at a time, as an oriole flies through the air and spills a gem of gold here and another there, up through the garden it kept com-ing, closer and closer, little fragments of "Amaryl-lis." Then the upper gate clicked. There was a step on the walk and up the back porch. Then there was a call, "Dad! Oh, Dad!"

Wide-eyed, Amaryllis and John Forrester stared at each other. Then John Forrester cried, "Yes!" in one great, panting gust. "Yes, John?"

The boy's voice came clearly, "I had the rottenest luck! Just a yellow cur! Just a common yellow cur upset the whole thing, and I got left, Dad! And I don't know that I care so much. I was afraid to go all the time for fear Amaryllis might come and I wouldn't be here."

"Stay there!" called John Forrester. "Stay right where you are and tell me what happened."

"Well, not much of anything," said John Guido. "I made the boat and I was on the yacht with all my stuff, and I happened to run my hand in my pockets just as we were cutting loose and I found that letter you told me to post about the sale of your last picture. I told one of the boys to tell them to hold on a minute, and I ran across the gangplank to post the letter. He said he would go straight and tell them to wait for me. He must have forgotten it or something, I don't know what. Anyway, I raced down the dock and I shoved the letter into the mail box, and as I turned, where men were unloading a freight boat, a big box fell down and landed right square on a little yellow cur—the commonest little cur that ever homed around a dock. One of the men laughed when the cur's head stuck out and he howled; and I couldn't stand it. I forgot about the boat. I forgot everything. I got him out. One leg was broken. He held it up, and before I knew what I was doing, I had broken some splinters from the box—I had no knife—and I had torn up my handkerchief and I was so busy making some splints and setting his leg and binding it up that I didn't realize how long I was taking. I didn't know they would go. I thought they would wait for me; but when I got him fixed and set him down and started back, the place where the boat had been was vacant. I ran with all my might, but that yacht was away out on the ocean. Its sails were up and it was going like a white bird. I could not make anybody see me or hear me, and I couldn't find anything I could hire to overtake it. I was so disappointed I sat down on a post and I bet I cried. I bet I cried like a spanked baby!

"Then, on a sudden, I remembered that I had not wanted to go so very badly anyway, and maybe Amaryllis would come. So I went back and I hunted up the yellow cur and I took him up in my arms and I walked all the way back. I walked all night. I just didn't want to hire anything, and I didn't want to ride. I'm all tired out and I'm hungry, and so is the dog. He got pretty heavy before the night was over, but I got him here safe where I can take care of him. I've got to make a better splint to fix this yellow cur so he won't be lame all his life. He wasn't anyone's dog, so I just made him ours. Won't you call Marie and ask her to get me some lunch pretty quick—real food? I'm tired and dirty and ravenous."

As they listened, John Forrester had been using his handkerchief. He had been wiping Amaryllis' eyes. He had been clumsily trying to straighten her curls. He had been pulling her blouse into shape and she had been standing dumbly cutting her fingers into his arms, her eyes torn wide open, her mouth hanging open, too. He was not sure that she had heard. He was not sure that she had understood very much more than that John Guido was on the back porch telling about a little yellow cur with a broken leg. He gripped her shoulders tightly and gave her a quick shake. He used her father's pet name for her.

"Amarylly," he whispered, "do you *hear?* Do you understand that John Guido is here?"

Amaryllis nodded and clung tighter.

Then came the voice of John Guido again,

"Father, will you fix a bath for me? I'm in the awfullest mess! Couldn't always see where I was going in the night. Got off the road sometimes, and this yellow cur wasn't any too clean to begin with. He must have a bath, too. But I want mine first, and food—real food. Then, Father, I'm going down to that wonderful bench with little loves all over it by the striped grass bed, and I am going to sit there until Amaryllis comes. But I must be clean before I go, Father."

"All right. In just a minute," said John Forrester. "Of course, you couldn't go to Amaryllis unless you were clean—clean in your body as you have kept your heart and your soul for her, son. You did not hear any word of the boat, boy? You don't know anything about it?"

"Why, there wasn't anything to know," said John Guido. "They were skimming out on the ocean hitting up the coast toward Maine. They were going to put in at a fishing place Peter knew."

"All right," said John Forrester. "I'll be with you in a second."

He whirled Amaryllis around and gently pushed her before him through the front door and out on the veranda.

"Go around the outside way and wait until I get him inside," he said. "Then go down to the seat beside the white syringa and I'll help him get cleaned up and I'll tell him what he needs to know before he sees you. I'll send him to you as quickly as it can be done."

Then he gathered Amaryllis up in his arms and over and over he kissed her.

"My little girl!" he said. "My darling little girl! Believe me, you are going to have another father who adores you!"

Amaryllis put her arms around John Forrester's neck and clung there a minute, and then she staggered from his embrace and started toward the end veranda steps, steadying herself by a hand laid against the side of the house at each step.

John Forrester went to his boy and hustled him into the house that he might not see Amaryllis going down to the garden. When he had gotten him inside, he went to the bathroom with him and helped him, as he used to when he was a little child, with his bath and putting on his clothing, working so efficiently and so fast that John Guido looked at him in wonder.

"What's your hurry, Father?" asked the boy at last. "What's your hurry? I'm not *that* nearly starved and neither is the yellow cur. Your hands are shaking, and, my word! you've been crying!"

"Never mind about me!" said John Forrester. "Get into your clothes! By that time Marie will have the coffee that I ordered ready for you. There is something I must tell you."

So, because he was an obedient boy, John Guido slipped into his clothes. He noticed that his father had laid out his very best suit. He opened his mouth to speak about it, and then remembered that to change would take time, and his father really did seem to be in an unusual hurry, so he said nothing. He slipped on a blue shirt and the soft blue-gray suit. All the time he kept thinking, "What in the world is the trouble with Father?"

When John Guido laid down the brush from the

very last stroke on his hair, his father took him by the shoulder and turned him around and looked at him from head to foot, and then suddenly he laid his head on the shoulder of the man who was as tall as he was and began to cry, began to shake and to wrench until, in dumb amazement, John Guido lifted him bodily and stood him erect and said, "For God's sake, Father, what is it?"

John Forrester said, "My boy, do you know what you mean to me at this minute?"

John Guido tried to laugh.

"Well, I hope," he said, "I hope I mean something that you are, at least, not ashamed of."

John Forrester answered, "My lad, my little lad, at this minute you mean to me *Resurrection*. My son that was lost is found; my boy that was at the bottom of the ocean has arisen and come back to me safe and sound just because of the bigness of his heart, so like his mother's."

John Guido stared at him in amazement and said, "Why, Dad, what are you driving at?"

John Forrester said, "Guido, go to Marie and get a cup of coffee and then come into the living room." And he turned and left the boy.

It was only a minute until the lad was back with his father.

"I don't know how to go at this to be the least of a shock," said John Forrester. "Perhaps I might as well tell you in plain English. There is the morning paper. You see the headline. Something went wrong with Peter's boat. I don't suppose anyone will ever know what. They must have taken in the sails and been running on the engine, and there must have been an explosion or something; some dreadful thing happened in the night. The report came in that some little splinters and pieces, some wreckage and débris that would float, were carried to the surface. And there was enough of the name of the boat and a number to identify it. Nobody is ever going to know what became of that boat and the handsome young lads who sailed away so gaily in it."

John Guido covered his face and began to sob, too. His father went over and knelt beside him and took him in his arms and said,

"Now, John Guido, I'll tell you a secret. I'll tell you why I urged your going when I myself was so afraid that Amaryllis might come into the garden in your absence. The reason was because I made it my business at the time the police came after her to find out just who Amaryllis was. I never told you that I telephoned for them, and I never told you that I knew her name. But I have known all these years, and I have left it up to her, because I wanted to be sure what kind of fiber was in her. I did not like her father over the phone. I did not like him when he came after her, trying to babble about money, about the millions the child represented, as if every child is not worth all the millions he has to any man that is even halfway a father! But Amaryllis seems to adore him. I have kept tab on him a little, and he seems to have changed. He seems to have made her the right kind of a home after she ran away to search for love. That seems to have wakened him up to the responsibilities of a father. I knew who he was, and on the boat, when that young chap showed himself friendly and told his name, it did not take me long to connect things up. John Guido, the new friend you made, Peter Minton, was Amaryllis' only brother."

"What?" cried John Guido. "Peter Minton was Amaryllis' brother! And he and the other boys are at the bottom of the sea? Oh, my God!"

"Yes," said John Forrester. "That's it. There was a reason, John Guido, why Peter Minton sought you out on the boat and made friends with you. He received a cable before he started from a little sister whom he seemed to idolize, and she had asked him to find you, to make friends with you, to bring you into his crowd, to ask you to his home. She had cautioned him not to mention her to you, and so, when the report came, she had not only Peter to mourn for, but she thought you had gone down, too, and she thought it was because she had begged her brother to make friends with you and to take you. It was because I wanted you to be friends with him that I urged your going when I intended never for a minute to leave the house and the garden until your return. Amaryllis thought, in making a way to open her home to you, that she had sent you to the bottom of the ocean. So this morning there has been a shock, an indescribable shock for her."

"But, Dad," cried John Guido, "Dad, how do you know all this?"

Once more John Forrester took his boy tight in his arms. He kissed him from brow to chin as he never had before in his life. Great tears were running down his cheeks as he said,

"My heart is racked with anguish for the fathers and mothers of those other boys, but selfish as humanity always is, I am forced to say, 'Thank God for my luck! Thank God for the little yellow cur that saved you!' I'm going now and give it a bath and see if you've bandaged it right. It is going to be my dog, my own particular dog, to the longest day that it can be made to live. It is going to be laid away as if it were a human being when it cannot live any longer. And now, John Guido, if I were you, I would go straight to the garden."

John Forrester opened the screen and gave the boy a slight shove toward the back porch. John Guido crossed it at a sweep and took the back walk at another. He never stopped to open the gate. He flew over it, and with a rush he came to a halt at the white marble bench carved with cupids and fawns and flying doves and rose garlands. Lying on it, in a little heap, in a little stricken heap, in a soft dress as white as the marble, a dress that brought out the sunshine of the hair and the great blue eyes, there lay a grief-racked little figure. John Guido went down on his knees and took it in his arms. He sat down on the bench and laid the gold head upon his shoulder and brought his lips down to the cheek that was uppermost. He could not say a word but,

"Amaryllis! Oh, Amaryllis, have you really come back to me? Have you really come at last? And, Amaryllis, have you come to stay?"

Amaryllis could not speak at all, but she could hear and she could nod her head.

Then John Guido straightened her on his knees and took her head between his hands and pushed back the tumbled curls, and Amaryllis did the thing of all the world that she had declared she never would do again, because always she had remembered how perfectly shameless she had been as a child, how her little starved heart and her little starved lips had cried out for the warmth of John Guido's tender caresses. She held her face up exactly as she had when she was a willful, neglected little Hungry Heart running in hot rebellion on a race to see if somewhere in all this world she could find love.

She lifted up her lips, all quivering and stricken, and she looked at John Guido with tear-brimming eyes. She caught tight hold of him with both her hands and opened her mouth and said it,

"John Guido, I am hungry *again!*"